Books by Helena Stone

Dublin Virtues

Patience
Equality
Renewal

Single Titles

Little Rainbows
Scenes from Adelaide Road

Equality

ISBN # 978-1-78686-154-2

©Copyright Helena Stone 2017

Cover Art by Posh Gosh ©Copyright 2017

Interior text design by Claire Siemaszkiewicz

Pride Publishing

Published in 2017 by Pride Publishing, Think Tank, Ruston Way, Lincoln, LN6 7FL, United Kingdom.

Pride Publishing is a subsidiary of Totally Entwined Group Limited.

Dublin Virtues

EQUALITY

HELENA STONE

Dedication

This book is for those who have supported and continue to stand for (marriage) equality.

Chapter One

"For fuck's sake."

The red brake lights on the back of the car in front of him flared brightly for the tenth time in less than a minute, making Lorcan curse, his words reverberating through the Nissan as he hit the steering wheel hard with the flat of his hand. He glanced at the clock on his dashboard display and realized he had more than enough time, but the thought didn't settle his nerves or do anything to lessen his frustration with the stop-go traffic he found himself caught in.

Maybe it wasn't the traffic jam so much as the uncertainty surrounding the day and his upcoming reunion with Eric. Lorcan wasn't sure and couldn't settle his thoughts long enough to figure it out. Being stuck in a barely moving line of cars didn't help the tension building in his stomach.

He went over the details once more. If the plane arrived on schedule it would land in an hour. Getting from the plane to the arrivals hall would take Eric at least another half hour, which meant that even if Lorcan had to leave his car behind and walk from here, he'd still make it to the gate with time to spare.

The traffic in front of Lorcan started to move and he shifted his car into first gear before almost whooping out loud when he had to change into second. Fifty meters, one-hundred meters, third gear…fourth — much to Lorcan's surprise, traffic continued to progress, and a few minutes later the exit sign for the airport came into view. The closer Lorcan found himself to his destination, the harder it was to control his nerves. He had no idea how this reunion was going to work out. Lorcan was looking forward to his reunion with Eric as much as he was dreading it. Excitement and apprehension alternated, throwing him from butterflies in his stomach to nervous cramps and back again now that the thousands of miles that had separated them were almost reduced to zero. In just about an hour they'd be face to face, and Lorcan had no idea what to expect, no frame of reference to work with.

His memories once more transported him back to the night he'd last seen Eric. Lorcan and Eric had been circling each other for almost two months by then, ever since their friends, Troy and Xander, had first met and had subsequently hooked up. The farewell party Xander had thrown for his best friend and housemate had drawn to an end and despite the fact that Eric was supposed to have been saying goodbye to all the friends who had gathered, he'd spent almost the whole evening with or close to Lorcan. Even when either of them had been talking to others they'd always been aware of where the other was and who he was talking to. It hadn't been until the last guests had left, and Xander and Troy were cleaning up the mess, that Eric had literally cornered Lorcan at the front door.

Lorcan steered his car toward the entrance of the parking garage. The first floor was full, as was the second. By the time he reached the roof and found a spot, he knew he should have saved himself the hassle of checking the lower levels. At least it wasn't raining. In fact, it was a very nice day for late March. After a long and mostly gray winter it was at last possible to believe spring would be brightening the world before too long. He rested his head against the support behind him and closed his eyes as the moment came back with such clarity he could almost feel and taste it.

He leaned into the door, handle pressing into his side, trapped by Eric's bigger and taller body only inches from his. His heart thundered as his mouth went dry. The look of pure hunger in Eric's eyes as he licked his lips stole his breath. When Eric bent forward and teased Lorcan's lips with his tongue, a sensation of pure pleasure ran through his veins, leaving him weak and mesmerized.

Never before had a kiss affected him like this. Toe curling and boner evoking didn't begin to describe it. They clung to each other like two men hanging onto a raft for dear life in the middle of an oceanic storm. The kiss went on, getting deeper, more heated and urgent with every passing second. He had no idea how long their lips had been locked together when Eric pulled back and pressed his forehead to Lorcan's.

"Why did we wait until tonight?" Eric's voice held all the regret Lorcan experienced and he had no answer.

The vividness of the memory sent shivers down Lorcan's spine and had an immediate effect on his cock. Lorcan still didn't understand what had possessed him to go home that evening, even if they had promised to stay in touch before he'd left.

He took the lift down to the arrivals hall as he reluctantly admitted to himself that he did know why he hadn't stayed that night. Even then the strong attraction he felt for Eric had scared him. He'd thought three months might be long enough to lessen the pull, to bring him back to his normal level-headed self. He'd been wrong.

Lorcan found himself on the receiving end of quite a few bemused stares when he reached the arrivals hall, checked his watch and laughed out loud. Despite the traffic and torturous hunt for a parking space, he was still almost an hour early. Clearly his obsession with never being late had gotten the better of him yet again. Still, it was one thing less to worry about and, on the upside, the plane from Canada was still scheduled to arrive on time, so the wait wouldn't be longer than it needed to be. Lorcan walked to the coffee counter, ordered himself a large Americano and tried to settle into one of the surprisingly comfortable seats. He allowed his thoughts to roam freely as he stared at the people moving back and forth around him.

To say he had been disappointed when Eric had told him

he'd have to return to Canada for three months would've been a gross understatement. Long before that kiss, Lorcan had privately acknowledged there was a connection between him and Eric. Even the very first night they'd met for what should have been a purely business related chat, Lorcan had hoped they would find an opportunity to get to know each other better. Xander and Troy falling for each other and quickly settling into a relationship had taken care of that issue. What was more, from that first night, he'd been sure he wasn't the only one who couldn't deny the pull between them.

A frown formed on Lorcan's forehead as he recalled how they'd never acted on that attraction. They'd been content to just enjoy each other's company whenever the four of them had met up and when Eric had to be in Lorcan's workplace to oversee the interior design job he'd been contracted to do by Lorcan's boss. Back then, Lorcan had told himself Eric was simply keeping his professional and personal lives separate. The fact that they hadn't kissed until after Eric had finished working for Lorcan's boss, shortly before he had to leave for Canada, had seemed to confirm that impression. But maybe he'd been wrong. After all, he was nobody's prize. With his short, spiky dark-brown hair and average features, he rarely warranted a second glance. Why somebody as sophisticated and handsome as Eric would be interested in him was beyond Lorcan — almost as big a shock as the fact that he occasionally found himself thinking about Eric in a long-term sort of way.

And yet... Lorcan relaxed as the memory surfaced again. It had been Eric who'd instigated the kiss. Eric had insisted they stay in touch while he was gone. Most calls between them had been initiated by Eric and it had been him who'd first introduced the idea of using Skype so they could see each other while they talked. Eric had obviously been delighted when Lorcan had offered to pick him up from the airport. On the other hand, Eric hadn't accepted Lorcan's invitation to stay with him until he could move into a place of his own.

Lorcan watched the area in front of the arrivals doors and smiled when a young woman started running before the sliding doors had a chance to close behind her again, straight into the arms of an attractive man. The couple held on to each other as if they'd been apart for years—and who knew? Maybe they had. No matter what happened next, the chances of Eric running toward Lorcan to collapse into his arms were slim to none. And that was probably just as well. Lorcan might have come to terms with the fact he was gay, even be comfortable with it most of the time, but it wasn't something he wanted to broadcast to all and sundry. Especially since chances were the majority of people weren't ready to appreciate such displays of affection. Sure, things were getting better almost by the day, and Lorcan wanted to believe that the upcoming marriage equality referendum would further improve the situation, but personal experience told him that many Irish people clung to their beliefs and preconceived ideas as if they were treasures to be guarded.

Suddenly restless, Lorcan drank the last sip of his now lukewarm coffee, got up and walked to the small bookshop. It was as good a place as any to kill time. He didn't want to think about his parents and their attitude toward him, but as always, his thoughts had a mind of their own and attacked. Sure, his father had made it very clear they would never reject him, but he'd also told him they didn't really want to meet any partner of his, should he find one.

'What would the neighbors say, Father Brendan? How would we be able to hold our heads up while the whole town is talking about our son's sinful lifestyle? And what about the grandkids? How would we answer their questions?'

Just remembering their words made Lorcan's blood boil. His sister, Laura, had taken some of the sting out of the situation when she'd assured their parents that her kids knew better than to discriminate, but it hadn't made a difference. His parents had refused to change their minds.

The message had been clear. Lorcan could be exactly who he wanted to be, as long as he didn't do it at home.

When a government minister had come out as gay in January, Lorcan had hoped it might make his parents less judgmental. They'd always been supportive of the politician and Lorcan wanted to believe they wouldn't suddenly change their opinion based on his sexual orientation. He'd been both right and wrong. Their position had been that while they didn't think the fact that the minister was gay would affect his political decision making, they would have preferred it if he hadn't gone public with the news. Frustration ate at Lorcan as he wondered, not for the first time, how his parents managed to navigate their way through life while wearing blinkers.

Lorcan didn't really see the titles of the books he was staring at as he recalled how he'd all but begged them to watch Panti Bliss's *Noble Call*. He didn't know how anybody would be able to watch those poignant ten minutes and not understand why it was important to allow people to be who they were without fear of repercussions. They'd flatly refused and Lorcan had stormed out of the parental house when they'd told him they would never be able to take a man dressed as a woman seriously.

He glanced at his watch for what felt like the umpteenth time since he'd entered the airport and realized he'd somehow managed to miss the plane's arrival. Eric had touched down on Irish soil twenty minutes ago. Nerves and happiness renewed their battle in Lorcan's stomach as he strode toward the doors which would open to reveal Eric before too long. He pushed his way through the other people waiting until the barrier stopped him from going farther, and fixed his gaze on the entrance.

Forcing his parents and their negativity out of his mind, Lorcan concentrated on the last conversation he'd had with Eric.

"Are you sure you can put me up? I don't want to be a nuisance," Eric had asked.

"Of course I'm sure," Lorcan had answered. "I wouldn't offer if I wasn't. Besides, what else are you going to do? Move in with Xander again? Book yourself into a hotel until you find a place of your own?"

The grimace on Eric's face when Lorcan had mentioned Xander had been priceless. "I'm sure Xander would offer me his spare room again, but…"Lorcan hadn't needed the rest of the sentence. He had known that Xander would never leave his best friend stranded, but he'd also realized Eric might feel uncomfortable in the apartment Xander shared with Troy. Those men were as in love and demonstrative about it as they had been when they'd first gotten together. Eric would be welcome to use Xander's spare room again, but Lorcan was sure he'd prefer not to intrude on the lovebirds.

When Eric had agreed to consider the idea, Lorcan had been elated, convinced that Eric would end up saying yes. Now that the moment of truth had arrived, he wasn't sure what he wanted anymore. If Eric agreed to stay with him for the time being it would answer any questions Lorcan had about them. He couldn't decide what would be worse—to discover that they were indeed irresistibly attracted to each other, or to find that the pull between them hadn't been strong enough to survive three months apart. One thing Lorcan had no doubt about was that he would be hurt if Eric decided to move into a hotel. And that was just stupid. Lorcan didn't do love or relationships. He didn't need anybody in his life—he was more than good on his own, and yet…the rejection would be devastating. Of course, acceptance of the invitation would be terrifying.

He watched while people who weren't Eric entered the arrivals hall and made their way either to those waiting for them or toward the exit. He hated the insecurity he experienced. He hadn't been as uncertain about meeting another man since he'd been a teenager. This situation would have been easier to handle if Troy and Xander had been here, too. But when they'd called to say it would be impossible for them to make it to the airport on time, Lorcan had told them not to worry about it since he would be there anyway.

Of course, now he was the one worrying about it. Would Eric think it strange Lorcan had come on his own? Would he mind? And where would Lorcan end up taking him? His mind went into overdrive again when the sliding doors opened once more and Eric walked through them. All worries and nerves evaporated momentarily as Lorcan lost himself in the sight of the tall man who somehow managed to look distinguished and fresh, even after a seven-hour flight. Then they were back with a vengeance—he who always planned his life down to the minute details had no idea what would happen next, and he hated it.

Chapter Two

Eric stopped walking as soon as the doors slid shut behind him. He scanned the crowd waiting behind the barrier, searching for the familiar faces he expected to see. It was good to be home and if he had anything to do with it, he wouldn't be accepting anymore overseas assignments from now on. With the economic recovery in Ireland moving along at a surprising pace, local commissions should start coming in again. He'd had it with having to uproot himself on the spur of the moment because a client on the other side of the world suddenly decided he'd had a change of mind.

His gaze nearly passed over Lorcan. Eric had expected to see Xander and Troy here, too, but clearly they hadn't been able to make it. He ignored the fact that the idea of having Lorcan to himself for at least a few hours both delighted him and had nervous excitement shooting through his veins. Eric closed the distance between himself and Lorcan before coming to a standstill, drinking in the features of the man who'd only been a voice on the phone or a face on his laptop screen for the past three months. It had been too long.

"Hey! Welcome back." Lorcan looked and sounded nervous. His mouth did that quirky thing Eric had seen before whenever Lorcan was tense, as if his lips couldn't decide whether to smile or not.

"It's good to be home," Eric said as he took the last step separating them. After putting his bag down and letting go of the handle on his suitcase, he spread his arms and pulled Lorcan close in a tight hug. It was probably his imagination, but Eric could have sworn Lorcan relaxed in his arms. For a fleeting moment, Eric considered kissing Lorcan, but instantly rejected the impulse, no matter how tempting. Even if Lorcan would welcome a kiss, Dublin Airport wasn't the right setting for a move like that. Besides, Eric didn't want to take things for granted. Three months apart was a long time considering he'd only known Lorcan for a total of five, even if Lorcan didn't appear to be in any hurry to sever their current connection. If anything, Eric thought Lorcan tightened his grip on him as the hug went on.

"Yeah. It's good to be back." Eric softly spoke the words directly into Lorcan's ear, then reluctantly took a step back and gathered his luggage again. "Let's get out of here." Eric noticed the tension and uncertainty returning to Lorcan's features before he turned and headed for the exit.

As they made their way out of the airport and toward the parking garage, a somewhat uncomfortable silence settled between them. Eric searched his mind for things to say but everything he came up with sounded either stupid or irrelevant to him. Funny how talking to Lorcan hadn't been an issue while he'd been away. Connecting on the phone or through Skype had been easy and relaxed, even if Lorcan had rarely instigated those conversations. Surely it should feel more natural now they were face to face again.

"Jayses fucking Christ. Will you look at that? How's that not a rip-off?" Lorcan pointed at the amount visible on the display of the parking fee machine. "Seven-euro-fifty for the hour and a half I've been here. That's ludicrous." Lorcan continued grumbling while he searched his pockets for the necessary coins, eventually settling on feeding the machine a ten-euro note and waiting for change.

"Maybe they did it on purpose?" Eric suggested. "You know, warning unsuspecting visitors that they've entered rip-off Ireland and should prepare to pay through the nose wherever they go?"

"Wouldn't surprise me," Lorcan muttered before laughing. When Eric joined him in the laughter, Lorcan turned his head to glance at Eric and he breathed a little bit easier when Lorcan's nerves seemed to evaporate before his eyes.

They still didn't talk in the lift to the roof or during their walk to Lorcan's car, but the silence no longer felt awkward.

"So, not that I mind having you to myself," Eric said once Lorcan had started the car, "but what happened to Xander and Troy? Last I heard they were determined to be here, too."

Eric caught the quick glance Lorcan threw his way.

"They'd every intention of being here. And they told me to mention how sorry they are they couldn't make it and that they're looking forward to meeting up for dinner in a few hours. They're interviewing a possible assistant for Troy. Right now was the only time the man could make it and the way business has been picking up lately, they apparently can't afford to let the opportunity pass."

Eric allowed the news to settle. Of course, he'd known Troy's recently opened tattoo parlor was going from strength to strength, but he'd had no idea it was growing fast enough for them to be in a hurry to take on someone. His conversations with Lorcan and Xander had told him Troy's reputation was good and growing, but clearly both of them had understated the facts.

"That's great news. I'm so happy for him," Eric said. "When you told me all the details about how he ended up opening and running that business on his own, I worried. Things might be improving in Dublin again, but people are still reluctant to spend money on anything other than essentials. Then again…" He laughed. "I guess it depends on what you consider essential. I'm sure Xander was convinced he needed that tattoo of his when he got it. I just thought he was mad."

"Oh, me too." Lorcan's gaze flicked in Eric's direction again before refocusing on the road and the other traffic. "I couldn't believe it when Troy and Xander told me the full story. But you can't argue with the fact that it worked better than even Xander could have hoped…you little bollix. Use your indicator, yagobshite." Lorcan shouted at the driver of the black car in front of them while slamming on the brakes and narrowly escaped driving full speed into the bumper.

"For fuck's sake. What's wrong with people? Do they want to cause an accident?"

Eric watched Lorcan's face as his expression shifted from livid to angry and finally frustrated. It was one of the things he liked best about Lorcan. The man couldn't hide any of his emotions. No matter how hard he tried to stop it, his face would always express his feelings loud and clear.

"Have you decided where you're going to be staying, then?" Lorcan asked the question while keeping his eyes fixed on the road and where they were going. His tone of voice sounded almost nonchalant, but Eric thought he detected a concerned note underneath the words.

"Sort of, yeah. Carmel, my partner, has found me an apartment. I'll be renting for the time being, but there's a possibility I might be able to buy it in a few months, should I want to."

"Oh. Good."

Eric didn't know if it was his imagination, but Lorcan's voice suddenly sounded flat and lifeless. And since Lorcan was still focused on what was happening on the road in front him, Eric couldn't read his expression.

"But I won't get the keys until tomorrow, so if your offer of a bed for the night is still open, I'd love to take you up on it." Eric stopped talking. He had more news to share with Lorcan but he wasn't sure about all the details or how it would be received, so he decided to wait.

"Sure." Lorcan's voice sounded a bit livelier than it had a moment earlier. "I told you. You're welcome to stay with me for as long as you want or need."

"I appreciate it." Eric reached across the handbrake and squeezed Lorcan's thigh. He didn't miss Lorcan's quick glance at his leg, nor the small smile when he lifted his gaze and turned to Eric. Well, that answered the question that had been playing on Eric's mind ever since he'd boarded his plane in Toronto. He'd been sure the attraction between them was alive and well all through their telephone conversations and video calls. And yet, the moment he'd stepped onto the plane, doubt had assailed him. Maybe it was all in his mind. What if it was just wishful thinking on his part? Three months were a long time to stay attached to a man he'd only shared one kiss with. No matter how hot and more-ish the kiss had been.

The motorway ended and Eric drank in the familiar surroundings he'd missed while in Canada. When he'd first crossed the Atlantic because work in Ireland had dried up completely, he'd imagined it might be a place he could settle in. After he'd returned to Dublin, two years later, he'd known he would never be able to leave Ireland permanently. He'd missed the smaller scale of life. It was too easy to get lost and alone in most other countries. Compared to other cities, Dublin had a village feel about it, and while he realized that could be claustrophobic to some people, Eric enjoyed the fact that whenever he walked through town he was bound to meet at least a few people he recognized. It was time to re-establish roots in the place he would always call home.

"Did I tell you I started playing darts in Toronto?" Eric asked.

"You did? Are you any good?" Because they had stopped at a traffic light Lorcan turned and looked at Eric, surprise and delight written clearly on his features.

"Good? Fuck no." Eric laughed. "I'd say that takes more than a few months. But I'm not as useless as I was when I started. I even manage to not miss the board most of the time now. What about Xander? Have you and Troy converted him yet?"

The light changed and Lorcan didn't answer until he'd pulled off. "Xander is a surprisingly quick learner. He hasn't beaten either me or Troy yet, but I wouldn't be surprised if that changes sooner rather than later. But then, those two have a board put up in Xander's apartment and play regularly." Lorcan stopped at another red light and turned to Eric with an expression on his face he couldn't decipher, before returning his attention to the road. "It's great to have you two joining us on our darts nights. You will be coming along, too, won't you?"

Once again, Eric couldn't see enough of Lorcan's face to read his expression and his voice didn't give him any clues as to whether or not Lorcan might attach any importance to Eric's answer.

"If you're sure you'd like me to play with you. By the sound of it I'll be standing out only for my ineptitude."

"You'll learn," Lorcan said. "I'll help you if you'd like."

Again, Lorcan made it sound as if Eric's reaction to his suggestion didn't matter, but despite the fact he could only see the left-hand side of Lorcan's face, Eric didn't miss the way his mouth twisted when he stopped talking — as if he was trying to keep a rein on his expression.

"Yes. I would like that. I've enjoyed it the few times I tried it. I'm just pretty much useless at it. Maybe you can explain how I go about having the darts end up where I want them, too… Not happening for me at all so far."

Lorcan turned off the main road and twisted and turned his way through a succession of smaller streets. When he indicated and stopped in front of a gate, Eric recognized the apartment complex. It was pretty typical of the newer estates that had exploded all over Dublin in the nineties and noughties. But Eric liked this one. At least here they'd taken care of good landscaping as well as all the fire and building regulations. Not all apartment owners in Dublin had been as lucky.

He followed Lorcan up the external stairs to the communal front door and up another set of stairs to the first-floor apartment he owned. Eric glanced at the door opposite the entrance to Lorcan's apartment while Lorcan unlocked his front door.

"What are your neighbors like?" Eric asked, studying the door across the hallway once again.

"I barely knew them." Lorcan pushed open the door then turned to answer Eric. "And that's unlikely to change now. They moved out last weekend. Actually…" Eric peeked at Lorcan just in time to see him lower his gaze as he left the remainder of the sentence hanging.

"Actually what? Go on, I'm curious now." Eric pushed past Lorcan and walked into his friend's apartment.

"I talked to them when I saw them moving their stuff out and asked about their apartment. I thought" — Lorcan's voice got softer until Eric had to strain to hear the words — "if they were going to rent it out, it might be something for you."

"Oh, that's very good of you. I take it nothing came of it?"

"I'd left it too late," Lorcan said. "They told me they'd hired a management company to find them a tenant while they decided whether or not to sell the place. By the time I asked, the deal had apparently already been done and dusted." Lorcan opened door on their right. "This is the guest bedroom. You can leave your stuff here."

"Sure. Thanks." Eric stepped over the threshold and took in the bright, if bare, room. He pushed his suitcase into a corner and put his bag on the small table in front of the window through which the hazy March sunshine shone, and tried not to pay any attention to his thoughts and feelings. Of course he'd hoped that his reunion with Lorcan would mean they'd continue what they'd only barely started prior to his departure for Canada. But the one kiss they'd shared — no matter how passionate it had been — didn't make a foundation for more. Neither of them had even referred to that particular evening during all their chats while Eric had been away, so he had no idea where he stood, and the same would be true for Lorcan.

"So, do you know anything about who will be moving in across the hall?" Eric forced his mind onto other, potentially much happier subjects.

"No. The couple told me they weren't too sure themselves. Apparently, that's why they hired that company. They wanted the advantage of receiving rent without the hassle of actually having to vet and subsequently deal with whoever moved in."

Eric allowed the possible scenarios to play through his head. He could say nothing and just surprise Lorcan tomorrow. On the other hand, he knew he wouldn't like that if their roles were reversed. In the end the decision wasn't hard, if only because the expression on Lorcan's face when Eric revealed his news would tell him so much about what might or might not happen next. He'd draw it out a wee bit, though.

"Are you worried about who your new neighbors might be?"

Lorcan shrugged. "Not really. These apartments are surprisingly well sound-proofed. I had little to no interaction with the couple before they left and there's no reason to think I would be more involved with whoever moves in next."

"That would be a shame." Eric left it hanging there as he studied Lorcan's face, wondering how long it would take him to figure it out.

"Why do you say that? I can't say I ever longed for more interaction with my neighbors. It would be different if…"

Eric allowed the broad smile to stretch across his lips as Lorcan stared at him. Lorcan's expressions moved from confused to delighted and back to confused again.

"You mean?" Lorcan hesitated. "You're having me on, right? There's no way… Is there? You mean to say you're…"

"I'm sorry, I should have said something earlier but I couldn't remember the way the house numbers worked in this building so I wasn't sure until we actually got here." Eric took a moment to drink in the relief showing on Lorcan's face. "I'm looking forward to us being neighbors."

Chapter Three

By the time they walked into the restaurant where he and Eric were to meet Troy and Xander, Lorcan was ready to strangle Eric. The man had disappeared into the guest bedroom for a rest followed by a shower only seconds after dropping his bombshell and long before Lorcan had been able to think — never mind speak — again. When Eric had at last resurfaced, they'd needed to leave the house so they wouldn't be late for their dinner appointment, and Lorcan had decided two could play that particular game. He'd kept the questions swirling through his mind under wraps. The bemused glances Eric had thrown his way were satisfying. If they were going to talk about Eric's future living arrangements, Eric would have to be the first person to bring up the subject.

A waiter approached and asked about their reservation.

"Table for four, booked under Barrett," Lorcan said.

"Please follow me, you're first to arrive. I'll show your guests to your table as soon as they get here."

They both ordered a beer and picked chairs on opposite sides of the table. For several minutes they just stared at each other and Lorcan felt as he had when he had been a kid playing Don't Blink First with his sister. He'd always lost in the past, but this time he was determined not to be the one to give in.

Eric opened his mouth, as if to say something, then closed it again as he stared over Lorcan's shoulder at something happening behind him. When Lorcan turned, he saw Troy and Xander approaching, accompanied by the friendly waiter. After greetings, hugs and a lot of back-slapping—

all of which attracted attention from their fellow diners—the four men settled at the table.

"So," Troy said, "you're back for good now or are there more international adventures in your future?"

Eric shrugged. "I can't say for sure that I'll never have to travel in the future, but if I do, it will be for a few days. I've no intention of leaving for months, never mind years, again. I mean, it allowed Carmel and me to keep the company running when most interior designers went out of business, and I can't deny I've learned a lot and gained quite a bit of experience, but it's not something I'd want to do indefinitely. If something else comes up abroad and Carmel wants us to take it on, she can do the traveling."

"Really?" Troy asked. "I imagined the traveling and being able to live and work abroad would be a perk rather than a hardship."

Lorcan studied Eric's face as he listened, and caught the rueful smile before he answered.

"That's how I saw it too when I left for the first time. I was all excited and even thought I might make a permanent move if I liked Canada."

"But you didn't like living there?" Lorcan asked.

"No, that wasn't it. Canada is a great place to live and I can't say I was miserable while I was there." A quick frown swept across Eric's brow. "Not the first time, anyway." He studied Lorcan for a moment as if he was waiting for a reaction. "I discovered that I really missed Ireland and Dublin. I like life here. As much as I can get frustrated at our politics and the provincialism while I'm here, I miss all of it when I'm gone."

"And there I was all envious of you and Xander for all the opportunities you have to travel and broaden your horizons," Troy said while Lorcan tried to figure out whether or not Eric had been sending him a message and, if so, what it might have been.

"No, I get what Eric's saying," Xander said. "I don't know about you"—he turned to Eric—"but I found it got old very fast. The first few times I had to travel for a commission, both in Ireland and abroad, I was excited and fascinated to see these new places. But it all got boring pretty fast. There's never really time to play the tourist and investigate the areas. I'm usually stuck in meetings or in hotel rooms. Trust me, it's nowhere near as glamorous as it sounds."

Eric jumped in. "It wasn't quite the same for me because I didn't travel once I arrived in Toronto so I could familiarize myself with the place and meet people outside the job, but that only reinforced what I'd suspected even before I left. I'm a homebody. I love seeing other parts of the world but only on holidays, safe in the knowledge I'll be back in Dublin again after a few weeks."

Lorcan leaned back in his chair and allowed the conversation to flow without any input from him. He'd been abroad on holidays a few times and had enjoyed those weeks away well enough, but he couldn't begin to imagine traveling around professionally. As an accountant, he rarely had to leave his office—clients usually came to him. In fact, it wasn't something he'd ever thought about, but now that he did, he had to concede that like Eric, he preferred his home and the familiar surroundings too much to want to be away for any length of time. Maybe Eric had been trying to figure out whether or not Lorcan shared his attachment to Ireland when he'd studied him.

"I don't know. The traveling still sounds exciting to me." Troy clearly wasn't as easily convinced as Lorcan.

"Tell you what," Xander said, "once your shop is established enough for you to leave for a few days in a row, you come along with me when I'm out and about meeting clients. We'll see how much you'll enjoy it after a few of those trips." Xander smiled at his lover. "Having said that, I may discover traveling is actually a lot of fun when I don't have to do it on my own." He shrugged. "We'll see. Either way, it will be an interesting experiment."

By the time the first course arrived it was as if the four of them hadn't been apart at all. The three months that had seemed endless while Lorcan had been living through them, appeared to have evaporated as they all fell back into old patterns.

"So, how did that interview go today?" Lorcan asked.

Troy's face lit up. "I figure I may have struck gold with this one. His name is Chris and he's an Aussie. He has fifteen years' experience and came with quite an impressive portfolio. In fact" — Troy frowned for a moment — "he's so experienced and overqualified I felt compelled to ask him why on earth he would apply for a job in my small parlor when there's bigger and better known places all over Dublin. As I told him, I couldn't imagine anyone turning him away if he asked for a job."

"And?" Eric asked. "What was his reason?"

"He said he hoped that working in a smaller parlor would allow him more freedom to give the customers exactly what they wanted rather than what management deemed appropriate. He said all too often in the past, his creativity had been stifled by time constraints." Troy smiled broadly. "Considering that was the main reason Shane was able to convince me to undertake this venture in the first place, I have no problem with his motivation. I told him he had the job before he left again. He's starting two weeks from today."

"And who knows" — Xander winked at Troy — "once Chris is settled in, we may be able to go away together for a short trip. I'm not complaining, but I think we deserve a few days of nothing but sex and relaxation in the not-too-distant future."

As they all laughed at Xander's statement, Lorcan couldn't help reflecting on how wonderful it would be to have someone to plan weekends away with. The idea pulled him up short. Until recently, he had been convinced he didn't want or need a long-term relationship. But the more he saw of Xander and Troy together, the more he realized there was a lot to be said for coming home to someone who enjoyed Lorcan's company as much as he enjoyed theirs.

"So, when's the next darts game?" Eric asked while they were waiting for their after-dinner coffees.

"Oh, very eager," Xander teased his best friend. "You're that desperate to humiliate yourself, are you?"

"You're that sure I'm going to make a fool of myself, are you? For all you know I've spent most of my spare time in Canada practicing," Eric said.

"Have you? Really?" Xander pretended to be crestfallen. "I was sorta hoping not to be the one getting a beating for once."

Lorcan listened and smiled as his three friends slagged one another off. There had been a time when he'd worried that Troy entering a serious relationship would spell the end of their close friendship. He'd never been as delighted to be proven wrong as he was right now. He loved seeing Troy happy and relaxed with Xander and he couldn't deny that meeting Eric had been a nice bonus to that development. If only he had some idea what, if anything, Eric thought about him. Part of Lorcan was convinced that his interest in Eric wasn't one-sided. But he couldn't be sure without either asking the question or making the first move, and he didn't feel brave enough to do, either. If he'd misjudged Eric, such a move would make things awkward between them, and as a result, also affect the way the four of them interacted.

"So, next Wednesday works for all of us?"

Troy's question brought Lorcan out of his thoughts and back to the conversation.

"Wednesday is fine for me," Lorcan said. "I've got something planned for Thursday evening but the rest of my evenings are free."

"What are you doing on Thursday?" Troy asked.

"I'm going to a Yes Equality Ireland meeting. I want to volunteer for the upcoming campaign and meet a few of the people involved."

"Mind if I come with you?"

Lorcan stared at Eric. "Not at all. The more the merrier,

I'm sure. I've seen the polls and realize all of them are indicating the Yes vote should be a sure thing, but I won't believe it until the result is actually announced."

"Shit!" Troy looked annoyed. "I'd love to come, too, but Thursday evenings are late opening in the parlor and I do actually have bookings for that night. Do me a favor, would you?"

"Sure, what do you need?" Eric asked.

"Find out how to sign up when you can't make it to a meeting. I want to be involved even if I'm not sure how much time I'll be able to invest."

"Me, too," Xander added. "I'm not available on Thursday either, but I'm going to do what I can to get that referendum to pass. You never know. I may want to avail of that opportunity myself one day."

"Is that right?" Troy smirked. "You and who else?"

Lorcan and Eric howled while Xander managed to keep the affronted expression on his face for all of five seconds, before joining in the laughter.

Twenty minutes later they finalized their plans for a night of darts and beer the following Wednesday. After Xander and Troy said their goodbyes and left, Lorcan and Eric chatted about the Yes campaign, darts and a host of other subjects as they walked back to Lorcan's place together.

It wasn't until they were standing in front of the door to his apartment that Lorcan became aware of the tension in the air. Nerves made him clumsy and he fumbled with his keys, only managing to insert the right one into the lock on his third attempt. Eric's hand suddenly pressing against his lower back didn't do anything to make him less insecure.

"You know you're a bastard, right?" Lorcan turned and faced Eric as soon as both of them were inside and the door had been closed.

"What?" The shocked expression on Eric's face was strangely satisfying. "What did I do to deserve that?"

"Why did you wait so long before telling me we were going to be neighbors? And why did you disappear into your room as soon as you'd dropped that piece of information?" So much for waiting for Eric to broach the subject first. Lorcan needed answers and he needed them *now*.

"Oh, that." Eric looked abashed. "Well, I really was confused about the house numbers in this building. And then when I was certain we would be neighbors, I figured I should give you a few hours to get used to the idea." He grimaced. "Wrong decision, was it?"

Lorcan thought about it for a moment. Part of him wanted just to rant and rave, but it wasn't in his nature to be impulsive, so he took his time and came to the conclusion that Eric had a point. Whoever had numbered the apartments in this complex had done so according to a logic only known to themselves. Even after living there for two years Lorcan still hadn't figured out how it worked. As for needing time to get used to the idea—the fact that Eric had realized he'd need that only went to show how well he'd gotten to know Lorcan.

"You're not uncomfortable with the idea of me living across the hall from you, are you?" Suddenly Eric sounded uncharacteristically insecure.

"No, not at all. In fact, I like it." Lorcan smiled self-consciously, unsure how much he'd just given away. "And you're moving in tomorrow?" He forced the conversation away from what could have turned into a very uncomfortable direction.

Eric nodded.

"That's grand. I'll give you a hand so."

"You don't have to." Eric said. "I'm sure you've better plans for your weekend than helping me haul my belongings from the various places I've stored them in."

"No, I've no plans and wouldn't mind helping out at all."

"Thank you." Eric smiled and stepped forward, bringing himself closer to Lorcan. "It's good to see you face-to-face again. I lived for our calls and messages while I was away, but you're much better in the flesh."

Nerves bubbled up in Lorcan's stomach. "I am?"

"God, yes." Eric's exclamation sounded heartfelt. "I missed spending time with you. And I regretted not doing more of this before I left."

Eric took the last step, which brought him toe to toe with Lorcan, and leaned forward, pressing his lips against Lorcan's.

The tension left Lorcan's stomach as his body relaxed into the soft kiss. This was exactly what he'd been hoping for and also what he'd been telling himself not to get his hopes up about.

When Eric parted his lips and brushed his tongue across Lorcan's, he was more than ready to respond. Lorcan opened his mouth and dove into the tangle of lips and tongues. He'd replayed their first and until now only kiss so often in his mind. He'd dreamed about repeating the experience while telling himself it was unlikely to happen again. Now that it was a reality, the kiss was better than he remembered. He could lose himself in this mouth and tongue. Heat traveled through his veins and Lorcan didn't resist the urge to press into Eric's solid body when it came. He wanted him with a ferocity he couldn't remember ever experiencing in the past. When Eric squeezed his buttocks and pulled him closer again, Lorcan groaned into Eric's mouth, unashamed about sharing his longing.

Chapter Four

Christ, this is good. Eric had waited for this moment, hoping it would come. After every single phone call with Lorcan he'd put his hand to himself to relieve the heated tension that always built up, regardless of what they'd talked about. Their Skype sessions had been worse. More than once he'd been on the verge of suggesting they both get naked while on screen, but he'd stopped himself every single time. One kiss, no matter how memorable, was not enough to base assumptions on.

Lorcan groaning into his mouth got rid of whatever doubts he might have had. They were certainly on the same page. If the erection pushing against his upper thigh was any indication, Lorcan was as hot for him as he was for Lorcan.

Eric deepened the kiss, taking it from tender to the edge of aggressive. Three months of pent-up lust tried to make itself known through the demands of his lips and the strokes of his tongue. Eric's answering groan when Lorcan grabbed the back of his neck, pulling him closer and holding him in a death grip as if he had no intention of ever letting go again, was as passion-filled and needy as Lorcan's had been.

When lack of oxygen forced them to break apart, Eric looked into Lorcan's eyes and saw the heat he felt rushing through his body, reflected in Lorcan's blown pupils.

"More."

They said the word at the same time and grinned at each other.

"This way." Lorcan took Eric's hand and tugged him along. As soon as they'd entered Lorcan's bedroom, Eric shoved the man he wanted with a passion bordering on necessity against the wall and assaulted him with his mouth again — claiming, demanding, giving and taking.

Suddenly just lips and tongues weren't enough. Eric pushed his hand underneath Lorcan's jumper, prised his shirt free from his trousers and explored the naked skin he encountered before trying to get rid of the obstructing pieces of clothing completely.

"Oh, for fuck's sake." The shirt and jumper refused to budge, leaving Eric frustrated. Lorcan seemed to understand his exasperation well enough. Grinning, he stepped back and pulled the tops over his head in one fast move, revealing his naked torso.

Lorcan was everything Eric had imagined and then some. His slim and compact body was perfectly formed. Not skinny by anybody's standards, Lorcan's body displayed neither well-trained muscles nor fat. Eric drank in the sight while he explored every inch of skin available to him. Having Lorcan shudder under his touch was as enticing as their kisses had been, which reminded him...

Eric dove in again and reclaimed Lorcan's mouth, biting his bottom lip while tweaking his nipples at the same time. The lust-filled groan Lorcan rewarded Eric with went straight to his already pulsing cock.

Eric wasn't sure who initiated the next moves but suddenly clothes disappeared off bodies at the speed of light. Any thoughts he might have had of taking it slow and indulging in a gentle exploration of Lorcan's body evaporated as more skin was exposed.

As soon as both of them were naked, Eric stepped back and took a moment to drink in the image of Lorcan's body. He wanted to etch it into his mind so he'd be able to recall it with precision every time he closed his eyes.

Lorcan surpassed the fantasies Eric had entertained about him. His always unruly brown hair was messier than ever, with tufts standing up in random places. His normally hazel eyes were almost black as heat and arousal had expanded the pupils. Lorcan wasn't big or built, but his shoulders were broad, his waist slim and his legs long and muscled. Eric settled his gaze on Lorcan's hard, swollen dick and sucked in a stuttering breath. The length pointing forward and up, combined with the glistening he detected on top of the head, proved once and for all that Lorcan was as interested in him as Eric was in Lorcan.

Only when Eric raised his gaze to look at Lorcan's face did he realize he'd been subject to the same sort of scrutiny he'd put Lorcan under. Lorcan's gaze was still firmly fixed on Eric's hard and throbbing dick. Lorcan licked his lips, making Eric's cock twitch in response. The resulting spreading across Lorcan's face could only be described as lascivious.

"This was well worth the wait," Lorcan muttered the words as if they weren't meant for anyone's ears but his own. "Come here." He took two steps backward until his calves hit the bed and Eric followed, not stopping until he'd pushed Lorcan hard enough to make him drop onto the covers.

Lorcan spread his arms in a clear invitation, and Eric allowed himself to fall forward, making sure to catch himself before he crushed Lorcan. Naked skin connected with naked skin and electricity-like pulses rushed through Eric's veins. He captured Lorcan's mouth again and let go of all subtlety as he sated a thirst he hadn't known he suffered from, while their bodies moved against each other as if they had minds of their own. Groans, moans and muttered curses filled the room and Eric had no idea whose mouth they escaped from.

An unexpected push to his shoulder had Eric flipping onto his back and before he had a chance to catch up with proceedings he lost himself in a sea of sensation created by Lorcan capturing his cock with his lips. Sensual tongue strokes over the head and the tiny hole being prodded drove him mad. Eric lifted his arse off the bed, trying to find more, go deeper.

Lorcan took in more of his length, and all rational thought left Eric. This wasn't the first blow job he'd experienced but he couldn't remember it ever being this good. Lorcan bobbed his head up and down, taking more of him with every move, swallowing around him until Eric's balls tingled and he couldn't decide what outcome would be worse. He didn't want Lorcan to stop but he also didn't want his climax to arrive so shortly after they'd started. With superhuman restraint, he pulled away.

"Now I get to taste you." Eric didn't recognize the voice growling the words, unaware he could sound so needy and demanding.

Starting at Lorcan's balls, he licked his way up to the tip of Lorcan's cock before descending again. He sucked one testicle into his mouth and had to use his hands to keep his lover's lower body still as Lorcan writhed underneath his sensual assault. After giving the other ball the same treatment he concentrated on Lorcan's dick, licking and sucking until Lorcan was making incomprehensible sounds. Reluctantly Eric released him, unwilling to push Lorcan too close to the edge.

"What are you?" Eric asked, trusting that Lorcan would get his drift.

"Versatile." Lorcan's response was more of a sigh than a word. "But I prefer to bottom."

"Match made in heaven." The words escaped Eric before he had a chance to think about them.

"Music to my ears." Lorcan's grin was dirty and hot, and relieved Eric of any tension about the words he'd just used.

"Lube and condoms?"

Without a word Lorcan rolled over and opened the top drawer on his bedside table. Moments later the requested items landed on the bed. Not wanting to waste any time, Eric tore at the packaging and sheathed his cock in latex.

Lorcan had remained lying on his stomach and Eric leisurely took a few moments to admire the beauty of the two rounded globes, inviting him to touch and penetrate, while he coated his fingers with lube. With his clean hand, he stroked them while at the same time dragging a lubed finger from the top of Lorcan's crack to his balls. The frustrated sounds emanating from Lorcan as he ignored his hole were beautiful and enticing. Eric moved his finger up again, stopped at the entrance and drew slow circles around it until Lorcan's movements all but forced his finger to press down and in.

"Yes. God yes," Lorcan moaned. "More. Harder. Please."

Lorcan's demands and shameless need pushed Eric forward. He added a second finger and smiled when he didn't have to move his hand at all because Lorcan did all the work for him.

"Don't make me wait." This was no request but a demand, and one Eric was all too happy to comply with.

His instinct was to be careful, to slowly enter Lorcan, but that decision was taken out of his hands, too. Lorcan pushed back until all of Eric's cock was surrounded by the tight heat of his arse.

"Now ride me," Lorcan choked out the words while he continued to move his body as if trying to show Eric how it should be done.

"Pushy much?" Eric's laugh sounded strangled to his own ears as he responded to Lorcan's demand, let go of any restraint he might have had and unleashed himself on Lorcan's body. The friction, the heat, Lorcan's unending stream of sounds, half words and mutterings all fueled Eric's passion. He raised himself to his knees, pulling Lorcan with him until both of them were free to move together. He reached around Lorcan's side, taking the man's cock in his hand, and wasn't surprised to find it covered in pre-cum. He synchronized the movements of his slick hand with those of his cock until Lorcan was an incoherent mess.

His balls tingled and his muscles tensed, his orgasm waiting for him, just a few more thrusts away. The moment Lorcan tensed around his cock and cum spilled over his hand, Eric surrendered and allowed his climax to follow.

As he filled the condom, his only thought was, *Never as good as this.*

The clean up afterward was quick, almost clinical, and it was only when they were both lying in Lorcan's bed, underneath the covers with their arms wrapped around each other, that Eric realized they'd both wanted their separation to be as short-lived as was humanly possible.

Lorcan turned to Eric, smiling at him before placing a soft kiss on his lips. "If I'd known…but then again, well worth waiting for."

Instead of replying, Eric deepened their kiss. Lorcan was right. If he'd known they would be this good together, he would have pushed for it prior to leaving for Toronto. On the other hand, he had no doubt that three months' worth of anticipation and fantasies had only enhanced this first encounter. He couldn't wait to discover where they'd take their coming together next.

Jetlag, combined with food and alcohol followed by the most amazing sex he'd ever experienced drew him into sleep. Eric's last conscious thought was that he'd be a fool if he didn't hold on to Lorcan with all his might.

Chapter Five

Lorcan slowly opened his eyes, not sure what had woken him up, until he registered the arm around his chest, pulling him into the body behind him while what appeared to be at least a half-hard cock pressed against his buttocks. Closing his eyes again, he relished the closeness and the comfort he derived from it. There hadn't been a single uncomfortable moment after they'd shared their first kiss. Neither of them had raised questions about whether or not they'd sleep in the same bed, and they'd played into each other's needs so well the previous night it was hard to believe it had been their first time having sex. More surprisingly, he still didn't experience any awkwardness. Far from it, waking up with Eric wrapped around him in a big-spoon-like fashion felt natural, as if this was where Lorcan belonged, as if he'd come home.

He stiffened. That was a scary thought. Placing that much meaning on one night of sex — no matter how amazing the experience had been — was madness and asking for disappointment. And yet, the idea that this might be the start of a different sort of relationship scared him, too. Would he be able to do it? Could he share himself and his life with someone else?

"Are you awake?" Eric's soft voice sounded gruff from sleep.

"Yes. Good morning." Lorcan whispered the words in an effort to hide all his insecurities. Now was not the time to explore his numerous doubts.

"A very good morning," Eric murmured before placing a kiss on Lorcan's shoulder blade.

Just like that, all tension left Lorcan's body again and he allowed himself to relax into Eric's embrace. There'd been no awkward moments the previous night and clearly there were none to be had now, either.

"This is the ultimate way to wake up," Eric continued. "You realize we're a perfect fit, don't you?"

"Sure seems that way," Lorcan answered as he realized how right Eric was. Eric's knees had settled into the back of Lorcan's, his arm held Lorcan in place with just the right tension to make its presence known without making Lorcan feel as if he had been trapped, and the way Eric's now much harder cock rested against Lorcan's arse finished the picture beautifully.

Eric lifted his hand from Lorcan's chest and wrapped it around his morning wood. The delightful kisses, now combined with soft nibbles against Lorcan's shoulder blade continued and Lorcan's need rose again.

For a few long minutes, he lingered in the sheer comfort of Eric caressing him, until the need for more became stronger than the pleasure. Lorcan turned and stared at Eric's face. The usually immaculately groomed man looked quite different early in the morning. The hair Lorcan had only ever seen styled to within an inch of its life was now a mess and the stubble on Eric's cheeks made him resemble a maverick rather than a polished executive.

Any worries about morning breath slipped from Lorcan's mind as soon as Eric kissed him and he responded in kind. The kiss stayed lazy but grew deeper. The desire growing in Lorcan was nothing like the desperate need he'd experienced the previous night. This was a quiet longing for intimacy and closeness. Lorcan pushed Eric's shoulder until the man turned onto his back, and draped himself over the longer and stronger body, making sure never to interrupt their kiss.

He didn't stop the delightful play of their lips and tongues either when he reached for the drawer they'd returned the lube and condoms to before falling asleep. It took some maneuvering but Lorcan even managed to unroll the latex over Eric's now fully erect cock and coat it in lube without moving his mouth away from Eric's. It was hard to withdraw from the kiss in order to position Eric's dick against his hole, but as soon as all of his lover's length filled him, Lorcan found that delicious mouth again and resumed their kiss while he slowly rocked his body up and down.

The kiss seemed never-ending as they both stroked naked flesh and Lorcan kept up a smooth and easy rhythm. He had no idea how much time had passed when suddenly slow and easy wasn't enough anymore. All Lorcan knew was that Eric seemed to reach that point at the exact same time he did. Movements became frantic. Loud and inarticulate sounds filled the room before Eric came, followed by Lorcan only moments later. It wasn't until Eric had gotten rid of the condom and he rested with his head on Eric's shoulder that Lorcan realized that for the first time in his life, he'd come without any stimulation of his dick.

"Definitely the best fucking way to wake up ever." Eric articulated Lorcan's thoughts exactly.

"I wish we could stay here all day," Eric said minutes later. "But I have a house to move into and my father is coming to pick me up at eleven. He'll help me transport the gear I've stored in his garage. What time is it anyway?"

Lorcan reached for the phone he'd left on the bedside table. "It's just gone nine. I guess you're right. We should get up. But there's no reason for your father to come and get you. I'll drop you over and that way you'll have two cars on hand to transport whatever needs to be moved."

The moment Lorcan said the words he almost wanted to take them back. He'd spent one night with Eric and now he was volunteering to meet the man's family? What was wrong with him? What if Eric's family was like his? They would either have to pretend they were only friends or expect a cool reception at best while a shit storm couldn't be ruled out, either.

"You sure about that? I mean, there's no need for you to

drive all the way to Dunshaughlin. It would speed things up, certainly, but it's a big ask."

"You didn't ask," Lorcan pointed out. "I offered. And it makes even less sense for your father to come and pick you up only to drive back again to get your stuff. Unless your father is coming with a loaded car?"

"No, he isn't," Eric said. "In fact, I specifically told him to leave the packing and hauling alone until I was there." Eric studied Lorcan for a moment before smiling broadly. "In that case, if you're sure, I'd love to take you up on your offer. It would save time, it would mean my father is less likely to overdo things and it means I can introduce you to the rest of the clan. Well, those who still live at home, at least."

Suddenly Lorcan was lost for words. Eric wanted to introduce him to his family. *Introduce me as what?* The question burned on his lips but he swallowed it. The answer didn't matter and one night in bed together didn't mean they were now in a relationship anyway. *Jaysus, a relationship.* He couldn't believe he was seriously considering a long-term commitment to Eric. When had he changed from being convinced that he wasn't relationship material into a man who could see himself building a future with someone else?

"Tell me," Eric said with a smirk on his face. "Is your shower big enough for two?"

* * * *

Two hours and a long and very hot — in more than one way — shower later, Lorcan pulled up in front of a large detached house just off the main street in Dunshaughlin. Several times during the forty-five-minute drive, he had opened his mouth to ask Eric about his family. Were they okay with Eric being gay? Would they mind Lorcan coming along? Would Eric's family not prefer to spend time alone with the son they hadn't seen for three months? But he'd kept his mouth shut and his questions to himself. The Eric that Lorcan had gotten to know was a sensible and well-balanced man. Lorcan had to trust that Eric wouldn't have allowed him to come along if it would mean an uncomfortable situation as a result. Now that they'd arrived, though, he suddenly wasn't so sure anymore. What if Eric had misjudged his family and their expectations? Lorcan had no doubt that if he were to arrive at his parent's house with Eric in tow, they'd disapprove and wouldn't even try to hide the feeling.

"I realize it's a nice house," Eric's humor-filled voice broke through Lorcan's musings. "But it's not special enough to warrant that much attention and if we sit here any longer my parents are bound to think something's wrong."

"Sorry. You're right. I was miles away." Lorcan tried to shake off his worries, or at least hide them well enough to keep them from Eric.

"What's wrong?" The joking tone had disappeared from Eric's voice to be replaced by concern.

"Nothing's wrong. It's just…" Lorcan stopped talking because he had no idea what to say next.

"Just what?"

"Are you sure your parents won't be disappointed you didn't come on your own? After all, they haven't seen you in three months, either." Lorcan went with what seemed like the most logical and least embarrassing of his concerns.

"Mind?" Eric sounded surprised at the suggestion. "Are you having me on? You should have heard my mother on the phone when I told her I was bringing someone along who I wanted her to meet. In fact, I'm surprised you didn't hear her, she was screaming that loudly." Eric glanced at the house for a moment, a grin spreading across his face as he turned back to Lorcan. "See, that's her and my youngest sister" — Eric pointed to what appeared to be a kitchen window — "trying very hard not to look as if they're spying on us."

Lorcan laughed as relief flooded through him. Curiosity he could deal with. It was animosity he had an issue with.

"Okay. Let's do this and put them out of their misery." Still laughing, Lorcan got out of the car and waited for Eric to join him before hitting the lock button.

If Lorcan was still worried while they walked up to the front door of Eric's parental home, most of those thoughts disappeared when Eric briefly took his hand and squeezed it in full view of those who were spying on them. The rest of his unease vanished as soon as he met Eric's parents and youngest sister, Siobhan.

While Eric was all for going full steam ahead, filling the two available cars with his possessions and driving back to Dublin, his mother had other ideas.

"Nobody's going anywhere until we've all had a cuppa and I've heard all about your time in Canada and this charming young man you brought along. Come." She grasped Lorcan by the arm and pulled him toward a huge kitchen. "Sit yourself down and I'll get the tea."

Lorcan studied the huge spread of food on the table and didn't have the heart to tell her he wasn't much of a tea drinker. At least now he understood why Eric hadn't been worried about the fact they hadn't had time for breakfast after their extended shower.

"So, are you his boyfriend?" Siobhan stared into Lorcan's face from the opposite side of the table, curiosity clearly visible on her pretty features.

"I—" Not knowing what to say, Lorcan was very grateful when the girl's mother interrupted him.

"Missy, you can stop that now. You're not giving Eric's friend the third degree. He's a guest."

"I see some things haven't changed," Eric remarked. "I'll answer your question, Siobhan. Yes, Lorcan is my boyfriend." He glanced at Lorcan uncertainly before continuing. "And don't even bother asking me anything else, because that's all I'm going to tell you."

As Eric lowered himself to the chair next to him, Lorcan could only hope his face didn't betray his shock. Eric considered him his boyfriend? They were partners? He was torn between delight that Eric apparently returned his feelings and fear because he had no idea what it meant to be in a relationship or if he was even capable of successfully being in one. And clearly his face had once again betrayed his feelings, because why else would Eric suddenly squeeze his thigh in what could only be described as a supportive gesture?

"This is amazing, Mrs. Kavanagh." Lorcan indicated the combination of sweet and savory items in front of him as Eric's mother at last joined them at the table.

"Please call me Joan," she said. "Mrs. Kavanagh just makes me sound old."

Lorcan studied the beautiful woman — who didn't look a day over forty, although she had to be — and laughed.

"And I'm Michael," Eric's father added. "We're not very big on formalities here and if you're going to be a regular feature, you might as well fit in."

Lorcan felt as if he was riding a rollercoaster, being driven from shock to shock. His parents would never allow anybody not of their generation to call them by their first name, unless it was preceded by either Aunt or Uncle. He might as well have stepped into a different world.

"Actually," Siobhan said, "I do have another question."

"I'm warning you," Eric responded.

"No, not about Lorcan being your boyfriend." She hesitated. "Well, not directly anyway."

"Okaaay." Eric sounded reluctant and not entirely sure about what might be coming next.

"I was watching this video on YouTube the other day." Siobhan nervously glanced at her parents before continuing. "Panti Bliss's *Noble Call*. Have you seen it?"

"At least ten times." The words escaped Lorcan's mouth while a sensation close to jealousy bloomed up in his chest. *I can't even get my parents to watch that ten-minute speech and Eric has a teenage sister who does it without prompting.* Disgusted with himself, he pushed the thought away again, hoping his resentment would move along with it. The fact that the girl had seen it and now had questions was an encouraging development. That was how progress would be made. He needed to concentrate on the positive rather than continue to focus on his own negative experiences.

"Maybe not quite ten times for me, but yes, I did see it," Eric said. "What do you want to know?"

"Well she...he..." Siobhan hesitated and blushed. "What is it anyway, he or she?"

"She, when you're looking at Panti. Rory, of course, is a he." Eric smiled. "That's your question?"

"No, I was just confused for a moment." The girl shrugged. "She, Panti, kept on talking about checking herself, trying to control her gayness so that others wouldn't see it." Siobhan picked up her cup and sipped her tea, her gaze boring into him and Eric as she drank. "You held Lorcan's hand while walking toward the house. Does that mean you aren't scared of being seen?"

Lorcan studied the girl on the other side of the table for a moment. Clearly, she was nowhere near as silly as he had assumed when she'd first made the 'boyfriend' remark. He turned to glance at Eric, curious to find out how he would answer his sister.

"Here, in the front garden of the house I grew up in, I'm not afraid, no," Eric said after a few moments of uninterrupted silence.

"But you are afraid when you're anywhere else?" Joan asked the question this time, concern clear in her voice.

"Not afraid, as such."

Lorcan knew Eric was trying to stay as close to the truth as he could without worrying his family.

"But...?" Eric's mother prompted.

"But, I wouldn't be inclined to indulge in public displays of affection unless I found myself in a gay club or a similar safe environment."

"That's so unfair." Siobhan's emotional outburst confirmed that she truly was a teenager. "If I can kiss my boyfriend on the street, why shouldn't you be able to do the same?"

Silence settled around the table as three members of the Kavanagh family studied her.

"Shit," she muttered.

"Boyfriend, huh? Wanna tell me more about that?" Eric teased.

"Or me," Michael added. "But not now."

Lorcan couldn't help feeling sorry for the girl, who'd obviously given away far more than she'd intended. He didn't think she was in trouble but had no doubt she had one or two lectures about what was and wasn't allowed in her not-too-distant future. When he caught her eye, he winked at Siobhan, who grinned back at him, clearly already recovering from her slip-up and not worried about any consequences.

The rest of the meal was a combination of delicious food, lots of banter and plenty of laughter. And all the way through it one word buzzed through Lorcan's mind — boyfriend. *He called me his boyfriend.* By the time they got up from the table to fill Lorcan's and Michael's cars with Eric's possessions, Lorcan was so at ease with Eric's family that he found it hard to remember he'd only met them an hour ago.

They were more than halfway home before Lorcan found the courage to ask the question that had been burning on his mind and lips ever since Eric had used the word. "So, we're boyfriends, are we?"

Although he couldn't turn to look at Eric while driving, Lorcan was all too aware he had the man's — his boyfriend's — full attention. "You didn't mind me saying that, did you?" The slight insecurity Lorcan heard in Eric's voice was as rare as it was endearing.

"No, not at all. It's just…" Unsure exactly how to continue, Lorcan allowed the sentence to die there.

"What? I'm sorry if I jumped the gun. I probably shouldn't have assumed. I mean, if you're not comfortable with a relationship and have something less formal in mind, that's okay. Really, it is."

Lorcan considered Eric's words. He recognized the beginnings of hurt underneath them. And shite — it wasn't that he didn't want to be in a relationship, he just wasn't sure how to do that.

"You see." Lorcan took a deep breath. "I've never been in a relationship. I didn't see myself as someone who'd end up in a stable and long-term partnership with another man. I have no frame of reference. What do I do? How do I do it?"

Lorcan knew he didn't imagine the sigh of relief coming from his left.

"We do it whatever way works best for us," Eric said as he stroked a thumb along the top of Lorcan's thigh. "We'll make it up as we go along and figure it out together. Okay?"

As he turned onto their street, Lorcan glanced at Eric's face and gave him a quick smile. "You realize you're talking to the man who always has to organize everything to the last detail before proceeding, right?" He deliberated for a moment and continued. "I guess you've got a point, though. Especially since I've no idea how I'd begin to plan for something I have absolutely no experience with." *And something I can't find answers to through a quick Google search.*

Eric's father didn't stay once they'd emptied his car. "I'm sorry, lad," he said to Eric as soon as the last of his belongings had been carried up to the apartment. "I promised your sister I'd bring her to her friend's house at four, and if I don't go back now, I'll never make it."

"It's okay, Da." Eric hugged his father with an ease that was foreign to Lorcan. "You go. Lorcan and I will sort this mess out."

As soon as Michael left Eric pulled Lorcan into his arms and gave him a long and sensuous kiss. "Did that take care of your worries?"

Lorcan returned Eric's kiss before answering. "Yes. One thing I won't be worrying about again is your family." Lorcan was immensely proud of himself when he managed to get the sentence out without putting the emphasis on *your*.

Chapter Six

"Oh, for fuck's sake!" Eric looked on with disgust as yet another of his darts bounced off the wire and straight to the floor, wondering how he could possibly hit the tiny metal strips when there was so much more of the rest of the board for his darts to land in.

"Whatever practicing you did do in Toronto clearly didn't pay off, mate." Xander laughed. "Looks like it won't be me who's the big loser tonight."

Eric walked to the board, picked the fallen dart off the floor and retrieved the two that had managed to reach the target. A score of only nineteen was atrocious, even by his standards, but he refused to let it spoil his evening. He'd get the hang of it eventually. He wouldn't mind losing if it wasn't for the competitive nature of his friendship with Xander. For as long as they'd been friends they'd been trying to out-do each other. They'd almost always started from a level playing field. Right now, Eric knew he had a lot of catching up to do, but he'd get there. He couldn't wait for the day he'd beat Xander. He didn't even contemplate ever getting the better of Troy, never mind Lorcan. Those two were light years ahead of Xander and him.

He returned to the table and watched as Lorcan stepped up to the oche—which he'd discovered was the name of the line on the floor he had to stay behind when throwing darts. Lorcan made it look effortless, and yet it was clear his concentration was total. It was as if he willed the darts to certain areas of the board. Eric wouldn't have been surprised to discover that Lorcan could make a dart change course mid-flight just by the power of his thoughts.

"You make it look so easy." Eric sighed when Lorcan sat down next to him, having just scored another hundred points.

"Years of practice will do that." Lorcan smiled. "If you like, we could go out and play together some nights. In the end, it will all come down to you doing it often enough to get a feel for it, but I could give you a few pointers along the way."

"Sounds like a plan," Eric said. "If nothing else, I have to get to a stage where I can at least beat Xander. He'll never let me hear the end of it if I don't catch up with him before too long."

"Competitive much?" Lorcan asked.

"Me and Eric?" Xander, who'd just returned from his turn at the board, jumped into the conversation. "That's an understatement." He took a deep drink from his pint before continuing. "Mind you, that's not a bad thing. If it hadn't been for our ridiculous need to outdo each other, I'd never have gotten my tattoo and the four of us probably wouldn't be sitting here right now."

"Yes!" Troy's exclamation interrupted the conversation and Eric turned to see the man pumping the air with his fist. "Last game to me!" Troy walked back to the table, a huge grin lighting up his face. "I haven't lost it completely yet," he said, aiming his remark at Lorcan.

"Never said you did." Lorcan turned to his friend. "All you needed was to get back into the rhythm. You were always good."

"That's not what you said when you were winning all our games." Troy smirked. "You were only too delighted to rub it in then."

Eric sat back and enjoyed the banter. It was clear Troy and Lorcan's friendship was at least as solid as the one he and Xander had built over the years, up to and including the friendly rivalry. He'd been lucky. When he'd first moved to Canada he'd worried that it might lessen the bond between him and Xander. He couldn't have been more wrong. Not only had he not lost his best friend, he'd gained another one and found himself a lover, boyfriend, partner—the label didn't matter, all three were more than he'd ever expected to have in his life.

As if he could read Eric's mind, Lorcan put his hand on Eric's leg and left it there. Eric squeezed Lorcan's fingers in acknowledgment as he contemplated how they were still trying to figure things out. Deciding they were in a relationship was one thing. Figuring out how that would work in practice was quite another. Living in the same building but not together made things more complicated rather than easier, as he'd initially thought. They hadn't spent a night apart since he'd arrived back in Dublin. So far, they'd gone back to Lorcan's apartment because Eric's had still been in a heap of unpacked and unorganized possessions. But most of the mess had been stored away now and Eric hoped they'd spend the coming night in his place. He knew he was being silly but couldn't help feeling the relationship would become more real to him after he'd woken up next to Lorcan in his own bed.

"Tell me to fuck off if it's none of my business, but..." The serious undertone in Xander's voice brought Eric back to the conversation taking place around him.

"But what?" Eric asked. "Come on. Spit it out. Since when are you shy about saying what you think?"

"What's the story with you two?" Xander blurted out. "I mean, Troy and I were speculating about the pair of you even before you went back to Canada, but you seem very cozy now." Xander gave Eric and Lorcan's entwined fingers on Eric's thigh a thoughtful stare.

Eric turned to look at Lorcan, unsure what, if anything, his boyfriend would want to say, but Lorcan seemed happy and relaxed.

"Well, as Eric told his sister a few days ago, apparently I am his boyfriend." The slight blush on Lorcan's face was adorable and made Eric want to grab him and kiss him silly.

"Well, what do you know?" Troy leaned back in his chair

and studied Lorcan with an expression of wonder on his face. "I didn't think I'd live to see the day."

For the first time since they'd had the boyfriend conversation on the drive back from Dunshaughlin, Eric realized Lorcan really hadn't been joking when he'd said he had never considered himself relationship material.

"But how cool is that?" Xander asked. "I mean, you hear all these horror stories about life-long friendships fading when relationships come into play." He grinned. "I like our solution better — best friends partnering up with each other's best friends. It's sorta freaky as well as perfect, isn't it? You could have saved yourself the hassle of finding an apartment," Xander addressed his last statement at Eric. He wasn't surprised when Lorcan stiffened beside him.

"That would probably have been a bit hasty." Eric kept his voice as neutral as possible. The thought had crossed his mind, too, but he'd dismissed it almost immediately. Even if Lorcan had been perfectly comfortable with the idea of a relationship, moving in together based on one night of good — *no, scrap that, mind-blowing* — sex would have been madness. "I mean, even you and Troy waited a few months before taking that step. He could have moved in with you as soon as I went back to Toronto but instead you waited another month."

"Besides," Troy added, "living together isn't for everybody and a good relationship doesn't stand or fall based on whether or not you share a house."

Fully aware that Troy had known Lorcan a lot longer and better than he did, Eric allowed the words to sink in, while wondering how he would react if it turned out Lorcan would never want them to move in together. He had no idea how to answer that question. The set up as it was now worked for them but he couldn't predict if that would change any more than he could predict next summer's weather.

"It's early days," Eric said, because he could still feel the tension radiating off Lorcan. "I mean, four days together is not enough to base our future lives on. We'll figure it out."

Lorcan squeezed their entwined fingers so hard it almost hurt before relaxing his grip, reassuring Eric that he'd given the right answer. They'd need to have this conversation sooner or later, but right now was neither the place nor the time.

"Yeah. Sorry." Xander looked somewhat abashed. "I wasn't entirely serious. You know me and my big mouth." He peered at Eric, who nodded. "I mean, there was more than one reason for me to get that tattoo." Xander glanced at his hand and the symbol for 'patience' taking pride of place next to his thumb. "I'm just glad you two figured it out. Troy and I could see it coming a mile off and you seemed to be oblivious to the way you gravitated toward each other."

Silence settled on the group for a moment, as if all their thoughts had returned to the month during which Troy and Xander had conducted their far-from-straightforward courtship, just as Eric's had.

"Are you two still going to that meeting tomorrow night?"

Troy forced the badly needed change of topic Eric had been frantically searching for.

"Absolutely," Lorcan answered, clearly far more comfortable talking about the upcoming referendum than relationships. "I want to be involved. I'm going to do whatever I can to help the Yes vote."

"Good. Make sure to get future dates from them. I want to be involved, too. And if you think there's anything practical I can do in the meantime, let me know." Troy paused and stared off into the distance for a moment. "Imagine if it did go through. I mean, that would be something, wouldn't it? Especially since this is Ireland."

"We'll get all the information," Eric said. "It's still early days. From what Lorcan told me, they only started the vote Yes campaign two weeks ago. And it's over two months until the actual referendum. I'm sure we'll have lots of opportunities to get involved. Anybody for another pint?"

When both Troy and Xander checked their phones for the

time, Eric realized their evening out was probably over.

"I'd love another one, but tomorrow is going to be one of those very long and even busier days, so I'd better not," Xander said. "It's nearly midnight. Time sure does fly when you're having fun, doesn't it?"

"I'm with him," Troy said.

"Color me surprised." Lorcan winked as he said the words, taking the sting out of them. "You two are right, though. I should call it a night, too." He turned to Eric. "Walk me home, handsome?"

"But that's so far out of my way," Eric deadpanned, raising an eyebrow for added effect. "Give me a sec," he continued while the others put on their coats. "I need to use the loo first."

"I'll wait for you outside," Lorcan said.

When Eric joined the other three on the street he saw Lorcan in what appeared to be a serious discussion with Troy. The conversation came to an end before Eric reached them and all he heard was Lorcan saying, "I'll give you a call tomorrow to arrange the details."

"What was that about?" Eric asked after he and Lorcan had said goodbye to Troy and Xander.

"Oh, just an idea I had. I didn't want to make a decision without running it by Troy first."

It could have been Eric's imagination, but he had the distinct feeling Lorcan was being more obscure than he needed to be. He opened his mouth to ask further questions before deciding to let it go. If it was important, Lorcan would probably tell him sooner rather than later. Besides, just because they'd grown closer over the past four days didn't mean Lorcan was under any obligation to tell Eric all his thoughts and plans. Troy and Lorcan had been friends much longer than he'd known either of them—just as he and Xander had been—so it was only natural they'd have things to talk about which had nothing to do with him...or Xander. And yet, none of that took the sting out of the fact that Lorcan wouldn't share his idea with him.

Fifteen minutes later, they found themselves on the landing between their two front doors. "Your place or mine?" Eric smiled while the thought occurred to him that he'd already started to take it for granted that they'd spend the night together.

"Yours. I think it's about time, don't you?" Lorcan turned to the left and waited for Eric to unlock the door.

Eric smiled in wonder as he realized that Lorcan might have picked up on his wish to spend the night in his new apartment. Or maybe just wanted to make sure they didn't slip into a routine he might not be comfortable with in the long term. They'd need to talk about their future sleeping arrangements—as well as a long list of other potential issues—at some point but, again, tonight was not the right time for those discussions.

"So, this is when I get to see the inside of your bedroom at last?" Lorcan turned to Eric while taking off his coat. "I still don't know why that had to be some big secret."

"Not a secret as such." Suddenly Eric felt silly about insisting he'd organize that room on his own. God only knew what Lorcan expected to encounter when he walked in. And while Eric quite liked his bed, it really wasn't the stuff of fantasies—sexual or otherwise.

Lorcan stared at him with a grin on the handsome face Eric couldn't imagine ever taking for granted. He pulled his jumper over his head before closing the distance between them and placed his hands on Eric's cheeks, kissing him hard. "Take me to your sex dungeon, sir."

Oh, shit. Lorcan's face had been too close for Eric to read his expression as he said the words.

Lorcan pulled back and studied Eric, his grin widening. "You appear to be very worried all of a sudden. You mean to tell me you've not been hiding a room filled with sex toys from me?"

Eric wasn't prone to blushing most of the time, but under Lorcan's amused scrutiny he could feel the heat rising up his cheeks. "No dungeons and no toys, either. I hope that doesn't disappoint you." He couldn't bring himself to say that he'd wanted to wait until the room was exactly as he'd envisioned it, just so Lorcan would only remember it as a place of comfort and pleasure.

"You're breaking my heart," Lorcan said.

If his face hadn't been so easy to read, Eric would have been worried.

"Come on, you bastard." He playfully punched Lorcan in the chest. "Just because there's no toys doesn't mean we can't have a good time."

Lorcan's expression grew sober. "I don't need toys to have a good time with you. As far as I'm concerned you're one big toy...made just for me."

Eric's heartbeat stuttered and he pulled Lorcan close for a long and heated kiss, stopping himself from blurting out something stupid, something that shouldn't be said for a long time yet, even if he had the feelings to back the words up.

Chapter Seven

"God, my mind is spinning from all that information," Eric said moments after they left the venue where the Yes Equality meeting had taken place. "But, wow, I'm impressed how organized they already are even though it's only been about a week since the official launch. And don't you agree it was heartening to see all those hetero couples? I was talking to this lady who told me she was there to support her nephew."

Lorcan listened and marveled at how Eric gave voice to the exact thoughts running through his mind. The meeting tonight had given him courage, and for the first time since the referendum had been announced, he allowed himself to hope it would all work out.

"I know. I was just thinking that if so many people whose lives won't be affected by the outcome are willing to turn their routines upside down in order to campaign for a Yes vote, we may actually have a chance of convincing the majority we need. I mean, even if every single gay person in Ireland came out and voted Yes on the day we wouldn't be anywhere near the numbers required. Adding on their families wouldn't get the numbers high enough, either." Provided those families were all supportive, of course. He hadn't asked them outright, but Lorcan couldn't imagine his parents voting Yes. His brothers and sister probably would, but the old folk? *Nah, that is never going to happen.* They were too caught up in their religion and would vote exactly as their priest told them to vote. Never mind that they'd be hurting one of their sons in the process.

"Hey." Eric grabbed Lorcan's arm and spun him around

until they were face-to-face. "Where did you just go? You look as if somebody kicked your favorite puppy."

"Sorry." Lorcan paused for a moment. He didn't want to talk about his parents now. He didn't want to share his suspicions with anyone, least of all Eric with his supportive family, until he knew for a fact that his parents wouldn't back him up. He couldn't escape the feeling that his parents' attitude somehow reflected on him. "I can't help worrying that we will need to convince a truckload of straight people to vote Yes on a subject that won't change their lives one way or another. I mean, even if they do believe we should have the right, will they come out to vote? What if it rains on the day?" The optimism he'd felt only moments ago evaporated and he hated himself for raining on Eric's parade. "We both know what the church is going to be saying about this subject. And there's still a lot of people in this country who will follow their priest's orders without a second's hesitation, just because that's what they've been doing their whole lives."

"All the more reason to get stuck into this campaign and not let up until we've secured our equal rights." Eric looked up and down the deserted street before planting a quick kiss on Lorcan's lips. "Never mind getting Xander and Troy involved, I'll be recruiting my parents and sister next time I see them. My father can put one of those stickers on his car and Siobhan better put a badge on her coat or there won't be any birthday present for her this year." He fell silent for a moment. "Mind you, convincing her shouldn't be a problem. I can't believe she'd actually seen the *Noble Call* video. Clearly there's more going on in her pretty head than makeup and boys." Eric grinned. "Don't worry too much. We can only do our best. And who knows, the people of Ireland may surprise us yet."

"God, I hope you're right." Lorcan tried to shake his dark mood but couldn't quite manage it. "You mind if we stop for a quick pint before going home? I could do with some liquid cheering up."

"Sure. I'm curious about that pub around the corner from us anyway. Let's check it out," Eric said.

They walked the rest of the way in silence. For the first time in almost a week, Lorcan couldn't come up with anything to say. Whatever he came up with in his head sounded either irrelevant or stupid. His thoughts veered from overly optimistic to deeply depressing despite his best efforts to change them. He glanced at Eric, who looked perfectly relaxed and at ease as he strode along. Lorcan wondered if he'd one day feel as secure in his life and certain about how he wanted to live it. Would he ever reach that stage? Would he ever be able to say, *'This is who I am and this is what I want and I don't give a fuck whether or not you approve'*? He got so lost in his dark musings that he would have bypassed the pub if it hadn't been for Eric steering him toward the entrance.

"Your usual?"

The question made Lorcan smile. Imagine Eric already knowing him well enough to realize he had a usual drink.

"Yeah, but I'd like a whiskey to go with it tonight."

Eric nodded after studying him for a moment. "Sure. I'll get them. You get us a table somewhere."

Finding a quiet table wasn't hard. The place was less than half full on this Thursday evening. It wasn't Lorcan's first visit to this pub and knew it was a safe and tolerant place. Still, he wasn't in the right humor to get into a discussion about marriage equality with strangers tonight. He'd get used to the idea of being vocal about the subject before he actually went out campaigning, but for now he wanted to be able to say what was on his mind without having to worry about whether or not he was offending others.

He watched Eric as he walked from the bar to the table where Lorcan was waiting, carrying the two pints and two tumblers containing whiskey with ease in his large hands. Lorcan suppressed the smile trying to reach his lips. Everything about Eric was large—body, soul and mind— and Lorcan admired every single inch of all of it.

The inclination to smile disappeared again as he wondered how to deal with all the feelings he'd been having. The way Eric was constantly on his mind, the emotions he experienced whenever they were together, or when he thought about the man or even when he just heard Eric's voice, were too new for him to be able to identify them. Was this what it was like to be in love? To love someone? It sure as hell wasn't like anything he'd experienced in the past, but that didn't make it any easier to put a name on it.

"You disappeared again, didn't you?"

Lorcan blinked and focused on Eric, who had somehow managed to put the drinks on the table between them and sit down without him being aware of it.

"I'm sorry, yes, I got lost in my thoughts. I'm not sure what's wrong with me. I'm switching from happy and optimistic to sad and scared and can't stop it."

Eric studied him, a thoughtful look in his eyes. "You are very invested in the outcome of this referendum, aren't you?"

"Yes, of course I am. Aren't you?"

"Sure. I want this referendum to pass. The inequality is ridiculous and a pain in the arse at best. That's not what I mean." Eric picked up his whiskey, took a sip and followed it with a long drink from his pint. "I would be disappointed and sad if we didn't get the Yes vote. Seems to me it goes much deeper for you. It's more personal for you than it is for me. Am I wrong?"

Lorcan opened his mouth to deny Eric's statement before closing it again. Eric was right, of course. It did feel personal and he would be devastated if the vote went the wrong way. It was different for Eric, because he knew that no matter what happened he would always have the support of his family. Secure in that love and acceptance, he didn't need the whole country to state their approval. Lorcan, on the other hand, wasn't sure about his family at all. He'd come out to them when he was twenty. After his parents had gotten over the shock, they'd informed him they would never turn him away but couldn't accept that being gay hadn't been a conscious choice he'd made. The words 'to spite them' had been left unspoken but Lorcan had had no doubt that was exactly what they'd meant. They'd added they weren't going to tell him how to live his life, seeing how he was an adult, but that they'd prefer not to be told about it and didn't want him to bring his lifestyle home to them. The painful conclusion hit him like a ton of bricks — he'd never bring Eric home to meet the folks.

He only realized he'd fallen into one of his silent, distracted episodes again when he became aware of Eric studying him, concern clearly visible on his face.

"I want to ask you what's going on inside that head of yours. The expressions on your face indicate some of it is very dark. I won't. I'm going to trust you'll tell me when you're ready."

A lump formed in Lorcan's throat and he took a deep drink from his whiskey, relishing the sensation of the liquid burning its way to his stomach. He didn't want to keep secrets from Eric, but he had to be sure first. Maybe his parents could be persuaded to change their minds. Maybe his siblings had shown so little active support for him because they didn't want to add fuel to the fire that could tear their family apart. Maybe... He had to get confirmation before he told Eric how different his family was from the close-knit Kavanagh clan.

"I will. As soon as I'm certain, I'll tell you." He hated himself for being cryptic, but it would have to do for now. "In the meantime, let's talk about practical things we can do during the campaign. I like the sound of that bus tour they're planning and wouldn't mind getting involved. Not full time, of course, but I'd like to jump onboard for one or two of the trips, at least."

"Yes, me, too."

Lorcan almost sagged in relief when Eric accepted the switch from personal to general without raising an eyebrow.

"I'm also going to talk Xander into creating some original

artwork. I'm sure he'd be happy to sell it and put the proceeds toward the campaign," Eric stated.

"You reckon he'd do that?"

"Absolutely. No doubt about it." Eric laughed. "You have no idea how hard it was to get him to understand that if he wanted to make a living from his art he had to stop giving it all away. I mean, anybody used to be able to ask him to create something and he'd do it, free of charge, just because he could and enjoyed it. Look at what he did for Troy."

"It took Troy ages to get used to the idea that Xander wasn't doing it as a favor or, worse still, because he was feeling sorry for him, but just because he enjoyed it and could." Lorcan remembered all the times Troy had told him how much he hated using Xander's designs without being able to pay him what they were worth. "And of course, now that the business has really taken off, Troy insists on paying him even though Xander keeps on telling him it's nonsense. Xander wants to become Troy's business partner now. He hopes that might stop the silly argument."

"Yes, Troy said as much. It sounds like the perfect solution to me. Of course, Troy is still hemming and hawing about it, but I'm sure it's only a matter of time. Those two were made for each other in every way imaginable." Eric laughed. "And to think that if I hadn't suggested that stupid bet they might have never met."

And if they hadn't, we might never have gotten beyond being business acquaintances. Lorcan kept those words to himself but wouldn't have been surprised if Eric's internal monologue mirrored his own.

The beer and whiskey did their job and Lorcan's dark mood lifted. All he could do was throw himself into the campaign and hope for the best. And he'd go home next weekend to talk to his parents. He'd have the conversation he'd shied away from when he'd come out, and get the answers he might not want to hear. Knowing exactly where he stood had to be better than this floundering around in the dark, second guessing himself and his family all the time.

An hour later, as he licked a wet trail from the base of Eric's cock to the beautifully swollen head before sucking it into his mouth, the thought crossed Lorcan's mind that while equality was important, *this* was what really mattered. With or without equality, Eric left him in no doubt that he *was* appreciated and wanted. It would break his heart if the referendum didn't bring the result he was hoping for, but Lorcan was certain he could be happy with Eric either way.

As if he could read Lorcan's thoughts, Eric bucked his hips, pushing his cock deeper into Lorcan's mouth. "God, yeah. You make me feel so good. Don't stop, please, whatever you do, keep going."

He would. Lorcan made the pledge in silence but meant every word of it. He'd never stop giving Eric pleasure and making him happy if he could possibly help it.

Chapter Eight

"Well? What do you think?"

Eric smiled when he detected the trace of uncertainty in Xander's voice. It never ceased to amaze him that even after a few years of successfully selling his artwork, Xander still didn't feel confident about his abilities. Clearly, some things never changed. Every time Xander created something new he still needed to be convinced it wasn't crap.

"Those are brilliant," Lorcan exclaimed. "Shit, to be able to create something as powerful as these." He pointed at the ten sketches stuck to the white wall in front of them. "And all in one day? You're something else, man."

"Thank you." Eric watched as Xander visibly relaxed. "They're not over the top, then? Or too sugary?"

Eric couldn't stop himself anymore and burst out laughing, only to laugh louder when Xander sent him an affronted frown. "Will you listen to yourself? When will you realize you excel at what you do? I mean, people wouldn't fork out thousands of euros for your art if it wasn't good, now would they?"

"That's all behind me." Xander waved his hand as if he had to physically push those works of art he'd sold into the background. "Just because people liked what I did yesterday doesn't mean what I'm doing today is any good. Hell, even the fact that they do pay for my work doesn't actually mean I'm good. It just means I'm fashionable right now." He glared at Eric. "Don't tell me you don't have butterflies in your stomach and aren't second guessing yourself whenever you need to show a design to a new customer."

Eric stopped laughing as he realized his friend had a point. He knew he was damn good at what he did, but Xander was right—there was always that doubt-filled moment whenever he introduced the ideas he'd come up with to a client. "Fair enough. Point taken. I apologize, but you're so…so—what's the word I'm searching for?—when you doubt yourself."

"Cute? Adorable?"

Eric turned to see Troy leaning against the doorframe with a grin on his face.

"He's the same whenever he designs a tattoo for one of my customers. I mean, he's usually there when they specify what they want. He shows them a choice of other pictures to see what they're into and still he's a bundle of nerves when he has to show the art for the first time. And I wouldn't mind, but every single one of the tattoos he's designed has been received with gratitude and endless amounts of gushing."

"Don't you start," Xander said, but the grin on his face made it clear he wasn't upset at all.

"Well, I think these are just about perfect." Lorcan continued to stare at the images as if the whole conversation had gone over his head. "Are you sure you want to donate these to the cause?"

"Duh. Yes? That's why I made them." Xander sounded perplexed. "What else would I do with them?"

Eric watched his three friends and just enjoyed the banter. This was what being at home meant to him. Of course he'd met people he'd gotten along with while he'd been in Canada. But those had been acquaintances at best. He felt safe with these three men in his life. He had no doubt he could tell them anything or ask them for support if he needed it, and they'd always be there. Sure, they made fun of each other, had a laugh at each other's expense, but underneath it all shone loyalty, friendship and—dare he use the word—love.

"What he means is," Eric decided to join the conversation

again, "that you could probably sell those pictures for good money rather than give them to a political campaign. Once you've handed them over they'll become public property."

"Yes, that's the whole idea." Xander had a determined expression on his face. "That's what I tried to express — the idea that equality is a public phenomenon. That equality doesn't exist unless it applies to everybody. See." He pointed at a drawing showing two couples with children. One couple was made up of two women, while the other portrayed the more traditional male-female combination. "What I wanted to get across is that it isn't so much about giving us special rights, but about allowing us to be exactly like everybody else. And that whether or not we marry or raise children doesn't affect the rest of the world, except that it makes it a fairer place. I mean, I'm sick and tired of people treating me different, as if I'm strange, a threat or, at the other end of the spectrum, special or exotic, exciting even."

Eric turned and studied Lorcan, who listened to Xander with what appeared to be total concentration, while his face displayed a sadness that punched Eric in the gut. He crossed the short distance between them and wrapped him in a hug from behind.

"Are you okay?"

"Sure I am." Lorcan's voice sounded almost normal but Eric wasn't fooled, especially since Lorcan refused to turn his head and look at him.

"One day you will tell me where all that anger and sadness come from." Eric whispered the words in Lorcan's ear, certain that his boyfriend wouldn't want the other two men to pick up on his feelings.

Lorcan sighed deeply before answering. "I will. It's no big secret. I just have to figure out how bad it really is first. Sorry to be so cryptic, but I can't tell you what I don't know for sure."

"It's okay. I just don't like it when you're miserable." It was a bit more than that, of course, but Eric didn't feel the need to add to whatever Lorcan's burden might be. He'd have to trust that Lorcan would tell him what was bothering him in his own good time. And if he refused to talk and also got more down-hearted, it would be early enough to apply some pressure. Eric was not going to be one of those partners who needed to know everything at all times.

"I think we're about ready to eat now," Troy shouted from the kitchen at the same time as a hearty smell permeated the air.

As Xander walked out of the room, Lorcan turned to face Eric. "Thanks for not pushing." He pressed his lips forcefully against Eric's.

"No bother," Eric answered when he had regained control over his mouth. "Let's eat. Something smells amazing."

The shepherd's pie tasted as wonderful as the aromas had suggested and for about ten minutes the only sound around the kitchen table was that of cutlery meeting plates and the occasional appreciative hum from one of the diners.

"I guess this is your handiwork." Eric addressed Troy. "Unless you managed to perform a miracle and domesticate Xander."

"Hey, there's no need for that." Xander tried hard to seem affronted but failed miserably.

"Are you forgetting I've known you most of your life and lived with you for a few months recently?"

Xander shrugged and laughed. "Fair enough. Imagine if I'd lost that bet. You would have ended up eating whatever I put in front of you for a month."

"And I don't actually need to lose weight," Eric said.

"Hey, he's not that bad." Troy rushed to defend his boyfriend. "He makes a very decent fry-up and is getting better at the rest." Eric watched as Troy turned a love-filled gaze on Xander. "Of course, your stomach and weight have nothing to do with my reasons for being delighted he accepted and then won that bet."

"I think all of us can be grateful Eric decided to pull me up on my behavior that night." Xander suddenly sounded thoughtful and serious. "Funny, isn't it, how what was supposed to be a silly challenge between two friends got us all together. And look at us now."

'Look at us now', indeed. Eric couldn't imagine a scenario in which Xander hadn't met and hooked up with Troy and, as a result, laid the groundwork for him and Lorcan to meet and get together.

"Did I tell you I took Xander home to meet my da the other day?"

"Really?" Lorcan looked and sounded shocked. "How did that go?"

"Much better than expected." Troy smiled. "You know what he's like. I mean, he didn't even approve of me hanging out with you, even though I'd told him more than once that we were nothing more than friends. I was prepared for, if not World War Three, then at least the cold shoulder, but he surprised me."

Eric swallowed his last bite of shepherd's pie and leaned back in his chair, his gaze fixed on Lorcan. Emotions flashed across his expressive face once again.

"So, what did happen?" Lorcan stared at Troy as if he wanted to draw the words from his friend's mouth.

"Nothing really. Maybe my having lived away from home for all these years made him realize he doesn't want to lose me completely. Or maybe he's mellowing down with age. I've no idea and I didn't ask." Troy laid his hand on top of Xander's on the table. "I mean, it's not as if he welcomed us with open arms and slaughtered the fattened pig, so to speak. But he was friendly, seemed interested in Xander and his art and actually asked us to come back again for another visit soon before we left." Troy shook his head. "You could have knocked me over with a feather."

"Your father doesn't approve," Eric stated.

"Well, he didn't, but it appears he's changed his mind. He all but told me to leave when I came out. It didn't really matter, because I was eighteen and about to leave for Dublin anyway, but it hurt." Troy shrugged. "But he seems to have gotten used to the idea. He really took to Xander and couldn't stop asking him about his work." Troy snickered. "I suppose he never expected his son to come home with someone famous."

Eric had been so engrossed in Troy's story, he'd almost missed the quick frown crossing Lorcan's forehead. *Bollix.* He really hoped Lorcan's parents were more accepting than Troy's father, but all Eric's instincts told him he'd just stumbled across the reason for Lorcan's dark moments. He opened his mouth to ask before thinking better of it. Lorcan had said he would tell Eric when he was ready. He just had to be patient. They hadn't been together long enough for him to start pressuring Lorcan.

"I've been lucky," Eric said. "My father has agreed to put a Vote Yes sticker on his car and to pushing them on most of his friends and colleagues as well."

"That's how it should be." Lorcan stared at his plate as he spoke. "You shouldn't feel lucky because your parents accept you as you are and we...Troy...shouldn't feel relieved because his father no longer rejects him. That should be the norm."

The hurt and anger in Lorcan's voice cut through Eric and appeared to affect Xander and Troy as strongly, if the sudden silence settling around the table was anything to go by.

Eric reached out to touch Lorcan at the same time that Troy did. Before either of them could make contact, Lorcan was on his feet and gathering plates and cutlery. "I'll take care of the cleanup, okay? It's the least I can do after that wonderful meal." The forced joviality was almost harder to listen to than the earlier pain had been.

Eric opened his mouth to say he'd help when he caught Troy shaking his head at him and mouthing, "Leave it be."

The evening never really recovered after Lorcan's outburst. They avoided the topic of the referendum after dinner and played video games instead. The joking and slagging one another off were as loud and ferocious as usual, but always with an undercurrent of care, as if the three of them had to tiptoe around a skittish foal. Eric wasn't surprised when Lorcan announced he was tired and wanted to go home at half past ten.

"Troy, can I talk to you for a minute before we go?"

Eric was shocked at the stab of jealousy he experienced when Lorcan asked the question. It made sense for him to want to talk to the friend he'd known for years, but Eric couldn't help wishing his boyfriend would turn to him about whatever bothered him.

"Welcome to the confusing world of relationships." Clearly, Eric hadn't been able to keep his emotions from showing on his face, if Xander saw through him with such ease. His words would have hurt if it hadn't been for the compassion in his voice. "Don't allow it to mean more than it does, Eric. Sometimes it's just easier to talk to someone you're not emotionally tied up with but who knows you almost better than you know yourself. You were there for me on the other side of the phone when Troy and I hit our rough patches. And I'm sure Troy talked to Lorcan about me a few times." He pushed a hand through his hair. "Hell, without Lorcan there might not have been a Troy and me. He'll let you know what's going on when he's ready. That's how it works for us, and you two won't be any different." Xander pulled Eric into a quick hug. "Trust me. This is familiar ground for me. I'm fast becoming an expert when it comes to relationships."

The attempt at humor was feeble at best, but Eric appreciated the effort so he forced a quick laugh.

"Thanks. I'll see you then." Lorcan's voice ended Eric's conversation with Xander.

"No bother. Just make sure you're sure." Troy's mysterious words did nothing to make Eric feel better, and neither did the almost complete silence between him and Lorcan during the taxi ride home.

"I'm sorry," Lorcan said when they'd settled into Eric's bed later. "I ruined the evening, didn't I?"

Eric pulled Lorcan closer in an effort to give him physical comfort where words wouldn't do the trick. "No. You didn't ruin anything. If you can't be yourself when you're spending time with friends, they're not the mates you thought they were." Eric wished he could come up with a way to relieve the tension he could still feel in Lorcan's body. "Oh, on a completely different note. Did I tell you I'm going to visit a hotel in Cavan next weekend to have a look around for a design they want me to do?"

"Yeah. You did."

"Well, they called today and offered me a room for the weekend. All expenses paid. Why don't you come with me?"

Lorcan fell silent and, if anything, became even more tense.

"You don't have to. It's only an idea." Panic blossomed in Eric's stomach and he tried to stop his mind from conjuring up an endless list of what-if scenarios.

Lorcan turned, placed his hands on Eric's cheeks and kissed him long and hard before pulling back again and staring straight into his eyes. "You've no idea how badly I want to say yes, and if you ever get such an opportunity again there'll be no stopping me."

Some of Eric's anxiety subsided again.

"But," Lorcan continued, "I have things I need to do next weekend. Alone." The beautiful hazel eyes were fixed on Eric's face. "No matter what happens then and regardless of the outcome, I'll tell you what's been going on with me when you come back from Cavan. I promise. Just give me until then. Please?"

It was the silent plea in Lorcan's eyes more than his words that convinced Eric. Whatever it was Lorcan had to do — and Eric had a suspicion he had a pretty good idea what it might be — it was clearly of great importance to him. Disappointed as he was that they wouldn't be spending a weekend in a luxurious hotel together, Eric couldn't bring himself to be selfish enough to either press for more information or insist

Lorcan should come with him.

"Sure. You do what you have to do. Just remember, if you need to talk, I'm only a phone call and under a hundred miles away."

"Thank you."

Lorcan's kiss was soft and sweet, as if, for the first time that evening, he felt completely relaxed. Eric allowed himself to drift along on the slow current of Lorcan's unarticulated apology. He could wait a little longer for his answers if that was what Lorcan needed. As long as Lorcan kissed him like this and fell asleep in his arms, Eric knew that whatever the problem was, it wasn't him. For now, that was good enough.

Chapter Nine

The closer Lorcan got to Killucan, the more he wished he'd never started his journey. Why he'd ever thought this might be a good idea was beyond him. It was, more than likely, the worst decision he'd made in a long time. He could have just left well enough alone. He'd managed to keep his family at arm's length for the past four years. Short and infrequent visits combined with weekly phone calls had been more than enough as far as he was concerned. He'd resigned himself to the fact that that would be the way of it. Why he suddenly needed to see if he couldn't rebuild some sort of relationship with them was a mystery.

He gripped the steering wheel more forcefully, tension making his shoulders hurt.

Except...Except that after he'd seen Eric with his family, Lorcan had experienced a yearning so strong it had almost brought tears to his eyes. He hadn't realized the pain he'd endured when his parents had told him they would never welcome a partner of his into their house was still as fresh and close to the surface as it apparently was. Then again, maybe it hurt more now than it had in the past. As long as the partner had been some sort of mythical creature he'd probably never encounter, it didn't really matter whether or not his parents would approve. Now that the myth had come to life, had a name and was so close to establishing himself in Lorcan's heart, the rejection stung like a bitch.

He checked his speedometer and hastily decreased the pressure of his foot on the accelerator. He tried to concentrate on the landscape flashing by outside the car, but the mostly still leafless trees did little to distract him from the thoughts running through his head.

It wasn't even as if he'd been yearning for a partner. Before he'd met Eric, Lorcan had been convinced he was better off alone. Not so much because he thought there was anything wrong with him, or because he didn't believe in relationships, but because living on his own had suited him so well. Until Eric, he hadn't been able to imagine why he might want to change his routines to fit somebody else into his life. After all, he'd never felt alone. In fact, he liked his own company and treasured the freedom to do what he wanted whenever the mood struck. From what he'd seen, relationships meant compromises and restrictions, and why would he volunteer for shit like that?

The sign announcing his exit from the motorway took Lorcan by surprise. It still scared him at times, how he could zone out during driving and suddenly find himself miles away from where he'd last been aware of his surroundings, without having any idea of how he'd gotten there. He indicated and decelerated, marveling, not for the first time, at how slow eighty kilometers per hour seemed compared to a hundred and twenty. Unless he got stuck behind tractors or other slow-moving traffic, he was only about ten minutes away from the end of his journey. He couldn't call the place where he'd grown up home. It wasn't. Not anymore. Home was his apartment in Dublin, now more than ever.

As he drove into town and slowed again he wondered what Eric would be doing right now in Cavan. Was he talking about the redesign the hotel wanted him to come up with, or playing golf, or maybe relaxing in a Jacuzzi? Turning into his parents' drive, he allowed himself to imagine sharing that Jacuzzi with Eric...naked. Blood rushed to his cock and he was torn between hysterical laughter and a deep-rooted shame at the possibility of entering his parents' house with a boner.

As he pulled up the handbrake the front door opened and an all-too-familiar man walked out. Lorcan sighed and contemplated just driving off again for a fleeting moment, before realizing it would not only be cowardly but also futile. His parents, who were standing in the doorway, as well as Father Brendan, had seen him. Leaving again wouldn't solve anything and would probably only make the distance between him and his family bigger than it already was. Reluctance made him slow, but Lorcan opened the door and stepped out of his car.

"Lorcan, my boy, I'm so glad I managed to catch you. I thought for sure we'd miss each other."

"Father." Lorcan forced what he hoped would pass for a friendly smile onto his face. "How are you?"

"Not too bad. Getting a bit slower, but sure, isn't that the way of things?"

Hard as Lorcan tried, he couldn't detect a trace of duplicity in the priest's voice. As far as he could tell, the man was genuinely pleased to see him.

"Your parents were just saying it's been months since you've been home. They miss you, lad."

"Yes. Well." Lorcan couldn't believe he felt the need to explain himself to the priest who'd had way too much influence over the manner in which his parents had raised him. "You know what it's like. Life gets busy and one week just blurs into the next and before you realize it, all that time has passed."

Father Brendan nodded. "Of course. But your sister and brothers still make it home regularly. Surely, if they can do it..."

It's none of your fucking business. The words screamed inside Lorcan's head and it was all he could do to not let them spill out. He had no doubt Father Brendan had been made aware of Lorcan and his sinful ways. And whatever else the man might be, he wasn't stupid. He understood perfectly well why Lorcan stayed away.

"I'm sorry, but unfortunately I can't stay. I would have loved to hear all about your life in Dublin. Maybe next time?" Father Brendan smiled and once again Lorcan had to admit to himself that the man appeared to be sincere.

"Maybe, Father. Who knows?"

"God bless you, son. Look after yourself."

"And you, Father."

From the frying pan into the fire. The words jumped into Lorcan's mind as he stepped aside to let the priest pass and glanced at his parents, who were still standing inside the open front door—both of them displaying somewhat smug expressions.

"Ma. Da." Lorcan bent forward and kissed his mother briefly on her cheek before shaking his father's hand.

"Come in, son. Dinner is about ready, and your granny is waiting inside. Did you have a nice chat with Father Brendan?" Lorcan's mother tilted her head, her satisfied smile suggesting that she'd more or less orchestrated the encounter.

"He asked how I was, Ma. About life in Dublin."

"Oh." For a moment, she appeared crestfallen. "That's all he said? He didn't mention—"

"Bridie, leave it be. Let the boy come in so we can all sit down and eat."

While his mother put the dinner on the table, Lorcan said hello to his grandmother. He loved her, always had, but he couldn't pin her down. She'd always been more of an observer than a participant in their family. She rarely volunteered her opinion about anything and had, as far as Lorcan remembered, never taken sides in conflicts—either big or small. She asked him about his life in Dublin and his job, but as always, he wasn't sure whether she was really interested or just going through the motions.

Half an hour later Lorcan had to admit to himself that, for all her faults, his mother still cooked the best Sunday dinner he'd ever tasted. He was tempted to open the button on his trousers after all the ham, mashed and roast potatoes as well as vegetables he'd eaten, but stopped himself. No doubt that would result in some sort of lecture about his behavior.

When his mother placed a slice of warm apple pie with custard in front of him, Lorcan knew he couldn't postpone the inevitable any longer. He'd come here for a reason — for answers. Unless he wanted to drive back to Dublin without them, he'd have to open his mouth and do the unthinkable.

"So." He hesitated and, for what was probably the tenth time since leaving Dublin, Lorcan wondered whether he should just leave well enough alone. Giving himself a mental kick in the arse he continued. "I wanted to ask you something."

His parents turned to each other and although nobody made a sound, Lorcan could almost hear his father say, *told you so.*

"The referendum. I was hoping you two" — Lorcan looked at his granny for a moment — "you three, are going to vote Yes in May."

"I can't believe you're asking us that. Voting is done in private here. It's nobody's business how we vote."

Lorcan was tempted just to let it drop again. While his father hadn't said no in so many words, his reaction made it perfectly clear that was where he stood. But, damn it, he'd come this far and he'd go the full nine yards, even if it meant widening the distance between him and his parents.

"I'm aware of that, Da. But this one is important to me. This referendum affects my life, my future. It is as if with this referendum the whole of Ireland is being given the opportunity to decide whether or not I'm an equal citizen. So, I want you to tell me where you stand."

Surprise flashed across Lorcan's father's face before his features returned to their usual neutral expression. "No, son, there's no way I can see myself voting Yes. I'm a good Catholic, and only this morning Father Brendan's sermon was all about marriage only being possible between a man and a woman." His dad sounded cool and matter-of-fact, as if the topic didn't involve his son's possible future.

"But what about equality? Am I not as good as the next person? Shouldn't I have the same rights?"

"Your father's right," Lorcan's mother said. "I'm aware all those activists make it sound as if it is about equality, but it isn't. Not really. Not for me anyway. You're comparing apples with oranges. Relationships between people of the same gender are never going to be the same as those between a man and a woman. I mean, if they really were equal, wouldn't same-sex couples also be able to have children together? The fact that they can't clearly proves God never intended them to be equal. Equality doesn't come in to it."

If his mother had slapped him, Lorcan wouldn't have hurt as much as he did. He'd expected them to tell him they'd never vote Yes. Sure, he'd hoped their love for him might be strong enough for them to ignore their church's rules for once, but deep down he'd known that would never happen. To have his mother tell him he wasn't equal to others in her eyes was a devastating blow he hadn't seen coming and wasn't sure he'd ever get over.

"Well, I'm voting Yes."

Lorcan stared at his grandmother in surprise. Where had the impartial and uninvolved granny he'd known all his life disappeared to? If he couldn't imagine his parents being on his side, he'd never even considered she might be. Judging by the expressions on his parents' faces, they were as shocked as he was.

"Mother." Lorcan's father sounded angry. "What sort of nonsense is that? You were there with us in church. You heard Father Brendan. Why would you go against his word?"

His granny studied her son for a few moments, as if she was weighing her words. "My faith and my church are important to me. My family are far more important. If voting Yes means I'm going to end up in Hell, so be it. I'd gladly burn if it means I get to support someone I love. Besides, I don't believe the church is right. If God didn't want there to be gay people, there wouldn't be gay people. It wouldn't be the first time our holy church got something wrong." With a snort, Lorcan's grandmother folded her arms across her chest and sent a 'take that' look at his parents.

"Well…I…" Lorcan's mother stopped talking, clearly lost for words and unable to comprehend what had just happened.

"Anyway," the grandmother said, "it's about time for me to go back to the home. Would you give me a lift, Lorcan? You're probably ready to go back to Dublin soon anyway."

"Of course, Granny." Lorcan smiled at the elderly woman he clearly knew nowhere near as well as he should, and got up, grateful that she'd given him a good excuse to leave straight away. He couldn't imagine spending more time with his parents right now. Not after what they'd just said. "I'll call soon," he told his parents. "I probably won't be able to visit for a while. I'm up to my neck in the Yes campaign until the referendum."

"Son, before you go." Lorcan's mother sounded sad. "I want you to remember that we love you. We'd never deny you or shut you out. We just think you're wrong. Surely we can disagree without it tearing the family apart?"

Lorcan swallowed hard before walking to his mother, embracing her for a moment and giving her small peck on her cheek. Much as he hated their attitude, he wasn't prepared to sever ties with the people who'd raised him the best way they had known how. If only disagreeing hadn't meant that they saw him as less than his brothers and sister, ignoring their opinion would have been a lot easier. So he didn't answer her question, deciding that she'd have to figure out for herself that his hug had meant he wasn't willing to give up on them yet.

A few minutes later Lorcan drove away from the house he'd grown up in after an awkward final handshake with his dad and with his granny sitting next to him in the passenger seat. He had no idea what to say to her. She'd taken him by surprise. The fact that it had been a happy shock didn't make it any easier for Lorcan to get his head around the whole thing.

"Your parents are fools."

Lorcan stared at his granny as if he'd never seen her before—clearly, she wasn't done shocking him. These words coming from the woman who'd told him to respect his parents no matter what they did or said for as long as he could remember, were unexpected to say the least.

"It's all well and good saying they don't want to cast you out of their lives," his granny continued, "but how comfortable are you going to be bringing a future partner home to them, knowing how they feel about you being gay?"

"I have one." The words escaped Lorcan and heat rushed to his cheeks instantly.

"You have a partner? Really? That's wonderful. Tell me all about him."

At least I think so. Lorcan ignored his sudden doubts, unsure where they'd come from, and spent the next ten minutes of their journey describing Eric to his grandmother. When he stopped talking—or had he been gushing?—she chuckled next to him.

"You love him."

"I—"

"Oh, it wasn't a question. It's as clear as day."

Lorcan parked the car in front of the retirement home his granny lived in and turned to face her. "You really don't mind at all?"

"No! Why should I? It's your life. I just want you to be happy." A small frown passed across her face, wrinkling her forehead. "The only thing I mind is that I don't have my own house and kitchen anymore. I would love to have you and your boyfriend"—his granny giggled—"over for dinner and get to know him."

Lorcan tried to get to grips with all the surprises he'd encountered in the past half hour. His granny giggling like a young girl only being the last of many. "If you really want to meet him..." Lorcan hesitated until his granny nodded. "Eric and I could come up together and take you out for dinner if you'd like."

"That would be wonderful," she said, enthusiastically clapping her hands. "And you'd better make it soon. I'll be dying from curiosity in the meantime."

"Sure." Lorcan laughed and shook his head in amazement. "I'll talk to Eric when I get home and I'll call you to arrange a date. Thank you." He whispered the last two words past the lump that had suddenly appeared in his throat. He leaned over and kissed his grandmother's soft but wrinkled cheek. "I love you."

"Love you, too, baby boy." She patted his cheek and smiled. "And don't worry about your parents. It may take some time but they'll come around."

As he walked his grandmother to her room, Lorcan reflected that he wouldn't be holding his breath for his mother and father to change their minds. Still, the day had turned out far more positive than he could have imagined, and for reasons he couldn't have seen coming in a million years, so who knew — maybe she would turn out to be right about his parents.

Chapter Ten

Eric stared from his own front door to Lorcan's and back again. He'd seen Lorcan's car outside, parked in its usual spot, so he knew he'd be at home. After the bus drive from the car rental company he could've done with some time on his own, never mind a shower. On the other hand, he had missed Lorcan. This weekend had been the first time they'd been apart for longer than a working day, and it hadn't been a great experience. It was hard to believe it had only been a few weeks since he'd returned from Canada and he and Lorcan had started their relationship. *I can't imagine Lorcan not being part of my days anymore.* The realization made him smile.

Muttering at himself for being an indecisive fool, he turned to his own door and opened it. Shower first, Lorcan later. He walked straight to his bathroom, dumping his weekend bag on his bed as he passed it. He allowed his clothes to crumple on the floor where they fell—they'd go straight into the washing machine as soon as he'd cleaned himself. He sighed in relief as the hot water hit his body while he reflected on what had been a successful weekend.

Well, except for having to travel there and back. Not that the hour and a half it had taken him to drive to the hotel in Cavan had been too much. It was the inconvenience of having to get to and from the car hire company that had done his head in. *I really must look into getting a car of my own soon.* He might not have a lot of use for it in Dublin, but having to rent cars for appointments elsewhere in the country was far from ideal.

Ten minutes later, feeling human again and dressed in

fresh jeans and a clean shirt, Eric let himself into Lorcan's apartment. They'd exchanged keys the day Eric had moved into his place without ever talking about it or turning it into a big deal. In fact, that had been the recurring theme of his relationship with Lorcan. It moved along almost of its own volition. They hadn't discussed what they were to each other beyond claiming the word boyfriends. In past relationships, there'd been long discussions about how they would be conducted and what was expected. None of that had happened with Lorcan and it felt natural. He liked that he and Lorcan just *were*, rather than trying to become something.

Lorcan wasn't in his living room and a quick glance into the kitchen revealed nothing but empty space. Eric moved on, only to stop walking when he reached the bedroom. Lorcan stood in front of the full-length mirror on his wardrobe door, his chest naked and stroking the skin on his left collarbone with his right hand.

Taking advantage of the fact he hadn't been detected yet, Eric allowed himself a few moments to observe the man he'd fallen for. Lorcan had the habit of putting himself and his appearance down, claiming he was average at best. Nothing was less true in Eric's estimation. Lorcan was as close to his idea of perfect as a man could possibly get. He adored the unruly brown hair, so much softer to the touch than the tousled mess suggested. The heavy eyebrows arching over expressive hazel eyes gave him a surprising vulnerability.

Eric enjoyed this opportunity to study his boyfriend's naked upper body. Slim but by no means fragile, Lorcan was everything Eric could have wished for in a partner and then some. The fact that Lorcan was about a head shorter meant Eric could truly wrap himself around his boyfriend, envelop him with his body. The fit was perfect as far as he was concerned. Eric shifted his attention to Lorcan's reflection and saw his presence had been noted.

"Like what you see?" Lorcan smirked.

"A lot." Eric walked into the room and did what he'd just been imagining. He wrapped his arms around Lorcan from behind and pulled him close. "What's with the fascination with your shoulder area?"

"I've been trying to make up my mind about this idea I've been playing with." Lorcan sounded nonchalant but his ever-transparent expression told Eric that whatever it was he'd been contemplating, it meant a lot to him.

"Are you going to tell me about this idea?" Eric kept his tone smooth, as if it didn't really matter whether or not Lorcan would share his thoughts, although the opposite was true.

"I've been toing and froing about getting a tattoo. I talked about it with Troy and he'll set it for me if I decide to go ahead. I know what image I want and everything. Until today I wasn't sure whether or not to go ahead and get it. I mean, I like them on others. Troy's sleeve is way cool. But to mark my own skin…"

Lorcan's gaze found his own and held it. "After today I'm certain I want to go ahead. I called Troy an hour ago. I'm getting it done next weekend."

Eric stroked his hand over Lorcan's left collar bone. The shiver running through Lorcan as a result of the touch was satisfying, but Eric didn't allow it to distract him. "It's going here?"

"Yes."

"And what exactly is it going to be?" Eric asked.

"You remember the tattoo Xander got?" Lorcan asked.

"Duh. 'Will I ever forget?' is a better question." Eric smirked. "I more or less caused him to get it." Eric raised an eyebrow. "You're getting the same one? You don't strike me as being in need of patience."

"No," Lorcan said, "not the same one. The same style." He placed his hand over Eric's just below his shoulder and squeezed. "I want the sign for equality, right here. Turns out that's actually two characters rather than one." Lorcan shrugged. "Who knew?"

"And why"—Eric hesitated before finishing the question—"did today help you make up your mind?"

"Oh, it didn't so much help, as made up my mind for me." For only the second time since Eric had met him, an emotion passed over Lorcan's face Eric couldn't put a name to.

"Gonna tell me about it?" Eric wondered if Lorcan could feel how fast his heart was beating.

"Yes." Lorcan turned around in Eric's arms and lifted his head before pressing his lips to Eric's.

When they came back up for air, Lorcan smiled. "Wanna sit or lie down while we have this talk?"

"Let's get on the bed." Eric grasped Lorcan's hand and pulled him along, effectively preventing him from picking up his shirt and putting it back on.

Eric made himself comfortable in the middle of the bed with his back resting against the headboard, spread his legs and tapped the space between his thighs. "Sit down and tell me about your day and how it decided you on getting a tattoo."

Lorcan settled where Eric had indicated and inhaled so deeply Eric could feel his body rising and falling again.

"Remember Troy telling us about bringing Xander home to meet his father?"

"Yes," Eric said, not at all surprised about the direction Lorcan's story was taking.

"Well, you're aware we grew up in the same town. We went to the same school and were dragged to the same church every Sunday. To be honest, Troy's father was worse than my parents. Troy was all but kicked out as soon as he finished his exams. My parents made a point of telling me they loved me and would never reject me."

"But...?" Whatever Eric had expected, it wasn't this. If Lorcan's parents hadn't rejected him or kicked him out, then what was the problem?

"I know what you're asking." Lorcan sighed. "My parents were and still are more subtle, or maybe I should say insidious. At least Troy had no doubts about where he stood. My parents were harder to figure out. They made it very clear they wanted me to be and remain a part of their family while at the same time telling me they would never welcome a partner of mine into their house and that I was to keep my lifestyle well away from their world."

Lorcan turned his head and gazed at Eric over his shoulder. "They made a conscious decision to put blinkers on. In fact, they embraced the 'what I can't see can't hurt me' attitude with great enthusiasm."

"Jaysus." Eric swallowed hard before continuing. "I can't even imagine what that must have been like for you. My parents never had an issue with me being gay. They probably figured it out before I did. And they were my fiercest champions whenever anybody tried to bully me or made disparaging remarks. Looking back, it's funny." Eric laughed softly. "They were so quick to jump to my defense, my school came up with a new anti-bullying policy just in the hope of keeping them away from the principal's office."

Lorcan leaned back into Eric's chest and stayed silent for a moment, as if he had to digest the information. "I can't picture that any more than you can imagine my situation. But, before you start feeling too sorry for me, it wasn't all bad. Like I said, I was never afraid I might be about to lose my family, and since I couldn't imagine ever being in a relationship with anyone, not being able to bring a partner home wasn't an issue, either."

Eric wanted to say something but he didn't know what to react to. Lorcan sounded so matter-of-fact, nonchalant even, as if his wasn't a sad story. He pulled Lorcan closer and spread his hand over Lorcan's still naked stomach, hopefully showing him he was close and cared, without having to use words. Silence settled around them while Eric decided there was at least one question he did need an answer to.

"Why were you convinced you'd never be in a relationship?"

"I'm not sure." Lorcan shrugged. "I just never saw myself as relationship material. It was easier not to have one when I was still living at home. Keeping a close relationship a secret was all but impossible in the town I grew up in. Later, after I'd first moved out, I guess I overindulged in casual encounters to make up for lost time. When the novelty eventually wore off I was so used to being by myself and doing as I pleased, I couldn't imagine what it might be like to share my life with someone else. I liked spending time with my friends, enjoyed the occasional hook-up, but I was too comfortable in my own company to ever consider allowing anybody else in."

When Lorcan fell silent again, Eric bit his tongue to keep from asking the question burning on his lips. Now was not the time to pursue that particular angle. He wanted to hear the details of Lorcan's day first.

"Besides," Lorcan continued, "I never met anyone I cared enough for to even consider confronting my parents about their refusal to ever meet a partner of mine. Of course, that was before I met you." He turned around and kneeled in front of Eric, looking straight into his eyes.

"See, that's why I had to go home today. Between Troy's father doing his turnaround, the upcoming referendum and easing into whatever it is we have together — no" — he pushed a finger against Eric's lips — "don't interrupt me — I had to talk to my parents and find out exactly where they stand and what it means for me."

The words 'whatever it is we have together' ate at Eric. Not because he was afraid Lorcan was less committed to the relationship they were building together than he was, but because Lorcan's uncertainty about his place in society broke Eric's heart. But Lorcan had asked him to stay silent, so he kept his mouth shut and waited for what was to come next.

"So, I went there this afternoon and when I arrived the parish priest was just leaving my parent's house. He was his usual interfering self." Lorcan hesitated. "No, that's not fair. He's not a bad man. Just very Catholic, if you get my drift. Anyway, long story short, I asked my parents if they would vote Yes in the referendum, you know, considering how they have a son who might like to get married someday. They gave me a unanimous negative response. Their faith didn't allow them to support their child. Not that they put it like that, but it's sure as hell what it boiled down to."

Eric's heart shattered as he tried to figure out how he would have coped if his family had rejected him — who he was — in the same way as Lorcan was being denied by his family. "Why aren't you angrier, more upset? I'd be kicking and screaming my frustration if I were in your shoes."

Eric wasn't sure what to think when a smile stretched across Lorcan's face.

"Oh, but that's not the end of my story." The smile widened. "Did I tell you my granny was there as well? Never mind, she was, and she completely took all of us by surprise when she announced she would be voting Yes because solidarity with her family was more important than anything the church could come up with."

"Thank God." The words escaped Eric and clearly amused Lorcan, who chuckled softly.

"That's one way of putting it, especially in this context," Lorcan said. "There's more."

"Okay, tell me the rest."

"She wants to meet you." A slight blush crept up Lorcan's cheeks and for the first time he looked away from Eric's eyes.

"She does? That's great, isn't it?"

"Are you sure?" Lorcan's question would have been cute if it didn't clearly show how insecure he was.

"Fuck yes. Of course I want to meet her, especially if she wants to meet me. I'd love to meet your parents, too, and give them a piece of my mind, but I don't imagine that would achieve anything except maybe make matters worse." Eric hesitated. "Can I ask you a question?"

"Sure."

"What about your brothers and sister?"

Lorcan took a deep breath and looked up at Eric again. "As far as I know my sister is on my side. She tore into my parents one time when they suggested that having a gay uncle might be difficult or harmful for her children. I have no idea where my brothers stand or what their opinions may be. We've never talked about it. How they might vote in the referendum is anybody's guess. When we talk, it's about all sorts of non-personal stuff, as if we're all avoiding the elephant in the room, know what I mean?

Eric had no idea what the situation Lorcan had just described might be like, but he nodded anyway. "So, when am I meeting your nan?"

"I was thinking — if it works for you — we could go two weeks from today."

"That most certainly works," Eric said, knowing full well that even if it hadn't been convenient, he would have changed things around until it fitted. He pulled Lorcan close and kissed him. He only meant for it to be a soft kiss, a show of support, but moments after their lips met the kiss turned deeper and hotter.

"I missed you," Lorcan said while he pulled back and opened first his own and then Eric's trousers. "For someone who couldn't see himself in a relationship, it didn't take long to get used to being with you."

"I'll take that as a compliment." Eric grinned while joining Lorcan in his efforts to divest both of them of their remaining clothes.

When they were naked and lying on their sides, staring at each other, Eric traced a pattern on Lorcan's left collar bone. "So now you want that tattoo?"

"It has been on my mind for a while," Lorcan said. "But when my mother told me the referendum wasn't about equality because we could never be equal to heterosexuals, well, she made my mind up for me."

"And you're getting it done next weekend?"

"Yeah, Saturday afternoon."

"Mind if I come with you?"

"Notatall," Lorcan replied in his best Mullingar accent. "In fact, that would be perfect, because Troy and I were saying how it might be nice to spend a night on the town afterward."

"I'm in." Eric's mind had gone into overdrive. It wasn't a decision to make on the spur of the moment, but with six days to play with the idea, he knew he'd come to a conclusion one way or another before Saturday. He wouldn't say anything to Lorcan until he had something to tell him, though.

"Come here." Eric turned onto his back and maneuvered Lorcan until the smaller man was stretched out on top of him. Neither of them closed their eyes as their lips met again, and Eric knew the heat in Lorcan's eyes was mirrored in his own. The kiss grew more heated. They stroked each other's naked skin and teased nipples until both Eric and Lorcan couldn't keep still anymore. Their joining was sweet and undemanding. Their hard cocks rubbed together as Eric and Lorcan's bodies moved in a slow but steady rhythm. Eric put his hands on the globes of Lorcan's arse and pulled him closer, creating more friction for their dicks in the process. Thoughts about Lorcan's parents, referenda and equality vanished until all that existed was Lorcan's body, Lorcan's hands on Eric's flesh, Lorcan's mouth devouring his and Lorcan's tongue tangling with Eric's.

They came almost simultaneously, not with loud shouts and groans but with deep and satisfied sighs. When Lorcan relaxed against him, the thought crossed Eric's mind that he should probably get a cloth to clean them both up, but he couldn't be bothered. The discomfort from the cum drying between them was nothing compared to the pure pleasure of just holding Lorcan close. Eric had no idea how long they lay there or what time it was.

"I feel like such a selfish sod," Lorcan broke their silence. "I never even asked how your weekend was."

"Never mind about my weekend." Eric kept his eyes

closed as he spoke. "It was good. It is a nice hotel and after I'm done with it, it will be even better. I got the job and next time I have to go there for a weekend, you're coming with me." Eric grinned. "My room came with this wonderful and very big Jacuzzi. It was wasted on just me."

Chapter Eleven

The little bell rang when Lorcan opened the door to Troy's tattoo parlor, bringing a smile to his face as it had done since the moment Troy had first installed it. It was such an old-fashioned feature in these days of modern technology and electronic surveillance. Eric followed him in and Lorcan heard the bell again as his boyfriend closed the door behind them.

"Hey, there you are." Troy glanced up from his work station in an alcove near the back of the parlor. He was working on someone Lorcan couldn't see while a young man with a messy head of dark hair looked on, standing so close to Troy that Lorcan wondered how he managed to get the job done. Before returning his attention to the client in his chair, Troy added, "Give me ten minutes and I should be done here. Xander's in the back if you want to go through and wait there."

"Sure," Lorcan answered. "Take your time. I'm not in any hurry. Any plans I have for the rest of the day involve you and Xander anyway."

As he passed through the shop to the door that would bring him to what used to be Troy's living quarters, Lorcan gave the workstation another glance. The black-haired youngster had a fresh bandage on his left hand. Troy appeared to be giving the occupant of his treatment chair a tattoo in the same spot while the darker-haired chap held his right hand. Lorcan couldn't help feeling the man in the chair was having a hard time. Given he was a redhead, the lack of color in his face might have been normal, but Lorcan was inclined to think it was more than that. The idea did nothing to settle the nerves somersaulting in his stomach.

He didn't realize he'd come to a standstill until Eric softly pushed against his lower back to get him moving again. Entering the space that had become Xander's official studio ever since Troy had moved in with the artist, Lorcan was surprised to see somebody with Xander.

"What's the story?" Xander peered up from the drawing he'd been working on and smiled at Lorcan and Eric. "Troy not ready for you two yet?"

Lorcan wondered about Xander's choice of words but before he could pose his question Eric approached his best friend and gathered him into a hug. Xander nodded when he and Eric separated again, as if in response to a question, although Lorcan hadn't heard anyone speak.

"Lorcan, buddy, how are you?" Xander pulled him into a quick embrace as well.

"Not too bad," Lorcan answered before staring at the fourth man in the room again. He was tall and broad, although by no means overweight. With short dark hair, a goatee and what closely resembled designer stubble on his cheeks, he was carelessly attractive. The glasses he wore gave him a slightly nerdy image, which disappeared as soon as he smiled.

"Oh, I'm sorry," Xander said, "Lorcan, Eric, meet Chris. Chris, these are the friends we've been telling you about."

"You're the Aussie," Eric stated while holding out his hand to the man mountain for a shake. "I guess a 'g'day, mate' is in order, so."

Lorcan cringed as he imagined how many times Chris had to have heard that particular line since he'd arrived in Ireland, but the man just laughed, shook Eric's hand and turned to Lorcan to shake his as well.

"You're happy here, working for Troy?" Lorcan asked. He knew Troy didn't need him to look out for him anymore, not now he had Xander by his side, but old habits died hard and, after the whole fiasco with Shane, Lorcan couldn't help feeling protective of his best friend.

"Yeah. Applying for a job here was the best thing for me." Chris's grin widened and he gave a very good impression of an ever-happy Australian. "These guys are amazing and it's wonderful to be allowed to just work without being scrutinized all the time."

"That's because you're good." Troy's voice came from the doorway behind Lorcan. "You don't need supervision. Fuck, you've been teaching me a trick or two and I thought I had the art more or less sussed."

"Works both ways." Chris gazed past Lorcan at his employer. "So, what do you want me to do?"

"Why don't you take Eric to the alcove on the right and me and Lorcan will take the chair on the left?" Troy asked.

"Eric?" Lorcan turned to his boyfriend. "What's going on?"

"I…em…" Eric studied his feet for a moment while a sheepish grin spread across his face. "I probably should have said something before now. I called Troy three days ago and asked him if there was any way he could give me the same tattoo you're getting today."

"You…What?"

"If you don't mind," Eric hurried on. "I mean, if you don't want me to get one, too, I won't. It's your idea."

Lorcan thought for a moment, assessing how he felt about the development. "No. I don't mind. I just don't understand why you'd want to do that. I told you about my parents and what it means to me…" He paused again, unwilling to go into details right now. "Your parents are so onboard with who and what you are, they can't possibly be your motivation."

"No," Eric answered, his earlier embarrassment replaced by confidence. "You are. Or, what you just said. Or both."

"But why?" Lorcan wasn't sure he wanted to be responsible for someone else getting a tattoo.

"Yeah," Xander jumped in. "I'd love to hear this, too. After all, you went to great pains to point out to me that tattoos are permanent when I got mine."

"I could leave and wait for you in the parlor if you want to have this conversation in private," Chris said. Lorcan decided then and there that he liked the Aussie. He was a refreshing improvement on that douchebag Troy had nearly partnered with.

"No, it's fine." Eric waved his hand in the air—clearly nowhere near as comfortable as he'd like them to believe. "It's not a huge deal. It is about equality, of course. About the referendum and what it would mean if it were to pass. But it is also about equality in general. It's my minor statement to the world that there are no better or lesser people. It doesn't matter who you are, what you look like, who or how you love or whether or not you are lucky enough to grow up in a supportive family. We are all equal."

Lorcan swallowed. Those last two sentences had been for him alone, although Eric had managed to make it sound as if that, too, was a general statement. He took the few steps separating him from Eric and stared into his eyes. "You sure about this?"

"Yes." Eric bent forward and gave Lorcan a quick kiss.

"Good." Lorcan's doubts evaporated. Eric was a grown man and he'd had a week to think this over. He couldn't help feeling that the four weeks they'd been in a relationship probably weren't enough to base matching tattoos on, but neither could he deny that the idea filled him with a lightheaded happiness he'd never experienced before.

"Okay. Let's do this." Troy walked past them into his parlor, followed by Chris.

Minutes later both Eric and Lorcan were bare-chested, with transfers of the characters for equality on their upper chests, when two tattoo guns switched on simultaneously.

"Fuck." Eric said the word as Lorcan thought it.

"Want me to stop?" Chris asked.

Lorcan was tempted to turn his head to make sure Eric was okay but feared it would interfere with Troy's work on his tattoo.

"No, it's fine." Eric sounded somewhat embarrassed. "It

took me by surprise, is all."

Lorcan closed his eyes and concentrated on his breathing as Troy's needle stabbed him. The pain felt appropriate. Equality, if they got it, would be hard won. It came on the backs of generations who hadn't even had the opportunities he and his friends had now—even without the possibility to marry. He was probably a sentimental fool and he would never say it out loud in front of his friends, but he almost wanted it to hurt.

"Hey, did I tell you those youngsters were delighted with what you'd done with their original design?" Troy's question—clearly not directed at him—brought Lorcan out of his self-indulgent musings. He wondered if he should be worried that Troy was talking while permanently marking his shoulder, before deciding that he trusted his friend and his long years of experience. He wouldn't talk if it messed with his focus.

"They were?" Xander sounded delighted with the news. "They didn't mind? After all, didn't they say one of them had designed it as a present to the other?"

"Yeah, something like that. But the guy who created it—I think his name was Aidan—couldn't stop gushing about the fact that his humble idea had been improved upon by the famous X-man. If he told me he was a huge fan of yours once, he told me fifty times."

Troy and Xander continued chatting, with Chris butting in occasionally. It didn't escape Lorcan's attention that Eric was as quiet as he was, while he allowed the conversation to flow over his head.

"Okay. That's you done."

The stabbing at his collarbone area stopped and Lorcan realized he must have zoned out at some point. He had no idea how long the process had taken. It didn't feel like much more than fifteen minutes, but he was certain that couldn't be right. He turned his head and looked at the chair a few meters away, where Chris took a step back and switched off his machine.

"And that's you finished, too," Chris said.

"Thanks be to fuck," Eric grumbled. "How you sat through having your whole arm done I'll never understand." Eric stared at Troy with a combination of admiration and horror clearly written on his face.

"That was not done in one sitting." Troy laughed.

"Makes it all the more amazing," Eric said. "I can't imagine volunteering for another session like this."

"We'll see." Troy winked. "You've no idea how many people have said that to me only to come back for more a few months later. Tattoos can be addictive. Even Xander has been talking about getting another one recently."

"What the fuck? Really?"

As Eric commenced giving Xander the third degree, Troy stepped around the chair until he blocked Lorcan's view and thus gained his total attention.

"Are you okay? You've been very quiet." Troy gazed at Lorcan with concern in his eyes.

"Yeah, I'm fine." Lorcan recognized the doubt in Troy's eyes. "Seriously. I'm not sure what happened. I sorta lost track of time. One minute you were drawing those outlines and the next you were done."

"Okay, that's not unheard of. Why don't you and Eric have a look at yourselves in that mirror" — Troy pointed to the left — "before we cover those tats."

Lorcan got out of his chair and walked to the mirror, physically aware of Eric following close behind him. When he raised his gaze and stared at the reflection in front of him, it wasn't his own collarbone he focused on. He stared at Eric's tattoo and yearned to touch it.

Emotions rushed through him, leaving him unsure exactly what he was feeling. In the month since Eric had returned from Canada, he'd never once second guessed what they were doing. All of it seemed to have progressed naturally, as if it had been pre-ordained. If he interpreted the mark on Eric's chest the right way, he and his boyfriend were pretty much on the same page emotionally. And yet neither of them had ever said the 'L' word or spoken about their feelings. They'd both waltzed into this relationship they were conducting as if it was their only option. Not that Lorcan had any regrets or doubts. He just had no idea what had happened or how to proceed. Then again, considering his experience when it came to relationships—none, to be precise—he had no way of knowing if their effortless coming together was the norm or something extraordinary. If what he'd seen of Troy's past interactions with boyfriends—or even the start of this current romance with Xander—was anything to go by, he and Eric were far from stereotypical. He should probably bring it up with Eric sometime soon, but that would happen in private, so he pushed the thought aside for now.

Lorcan almost laughed out loud when both he and Eric turned to face each other at the same time. Wordlessly they both raised a hand and traced a finger across the other's skin, circling the tattoo.

"No touching," Troy and Chris shouted as one and all five of them burst out laughing while Eric and Lorcan hastily withdrew their hands as if they'd burned their fingers.

"Seriously," Troy continued, "the risk of infection is too big. You'll have to keep your hands off that stretch of skin at least for the next few days. By all means check the tattoos for signs of infection and make sure they're clean, but don't go rubbing them."

"I know." Lorcan looked at his friend and nodded. "I read up on tattoos and how to care for them."

"Of course you did." Troy smirked as he joined Eric and Lorcan. "You wouldn't be you if you hadn't studied all the pros and cons before getting into this." He applied more disinfectant to the tattooed area and secured a gauzed bandage over it, while Chris did the same for Eric.

Lorcan shrugged. So he liked to have his facts straight prior to diving into new ventures. He'd always been that way and couldn't imagine ever changing into somebody more spontaneous.

Except that he hadn't been careful when it came to Eric. He'd taken the leap without giving it anything resembling serious contemplation and he still didn't question the role Eric suddenly played in his life. He had no idea whether that was good or bad, but Eric felt right. That was all that mattered.

"Okay, let's get this show on the road. We're due in the restaurant in just under an hour." Ever-practical Troy gathered the troops. "Give me a few minutes to change clothes and freshen up and we'll go."

"I'm off," Chris said. "Places to be and people to meet. See you Monday, boss." He turned and opened the shop door, setting the little bell off again while the rest of them shouted their goodbyes.

When Xander and Troy returned to the back rooms, Lorcan and Eric put their shirts on before turning to face each other again.

"Come here," Eric said.

Lorcan stepped into Eric's hug and rested his head against Eric's shoulder. A sharp intake of breath had him pulling back instantly.

"Are you sure you don't mind me jumping in on your idea?" Eric asked.

"Bit late to worry about that now, isn't it?" Lorcan grinned at Eric. "No, I don't mind at all. I like it, actually. But you could have warned me. I like a surprise as much as the next person, but this is taking it to a whole new level."

"Yeah. Well." Eric looked away for a moment. "To be honest, I wasn't entirely sure I'd go ahead with it until I sat down in that chair."

Lorcan opened his mouth to admonish Eric and closed it again. It was a bit late for that, too. The deed was done and he knew Eric well enough to be sure he wouldn't have gone ahead if he didn't want to.

"Well, I have to admit the possibility never crossed my mind," Lorcan said. "But now that we've both got one, I quite like it."

"Only quite?" Eric raised an eyebrow before smashing his lips against Lorcan's and invading his mouth.

Lorcan lost himself in the kiss while realizing that 'quite' had been the wrong word to use as well as a huge understatement. It was as if their relationship had taken a leap forward without any conscious effort on his part. Eric's decision made the connection between them stronger, more official. As soon as the realization hit him, Lorcan waited for the accompanying stab of panic he experienced whenever he allowed himself to acknowledge that he'd entered into a relationship, but much to his surprise he was delighted rather than worried.

"Okay, lovebirds, as much as we're enjoying the floorshow you're presenting, this isn't getting us into town. Break it up." Troy's laughter-filled voice brought Lorcan back to the present, and heat erupted on his face as he reluctantly stepped back from Eric.

Ten minutes later, when the four of them poured themselves into a taxi, Lorcan still floated on a cloud of wonder. His life was changing in ways he could never have imagined, and although not being in total control of the situation should have made him uncomfortable, he couldn't deny he loved it.

Chapter Twelve

"Your place or mine?" Lorcan looked up at Eric.

"Yours," Eric said as he marveled at how normal making this decision every single day had become. Part of him had been waiting for the moment Lorcan would start to feel hemmed in, but as days had turned into weeks and weeks into a month and it hadn't happened, he'd stopped worrying about it. Maybe all Lorcan had needed to overcome his reservations about relationships was just to be in one.

"I assume you've been your usual well-organized self and do have food in the house?" Eric asked. He'd been busy with a design all day and had completely forgotten to hit the shops. As a result, he didn't even have bread in his apartment.

"You mean you don't?" Lorcan smirked. "Color me shocked." He opened the door and led the way in, only a little shaky on his feet. Eric liked this tipsy version of Lorcan. He hadn't seen him like this before and might have had a sneaky hand in getting Lorcan to this stage of inebriation. Not that Lorcan was drunk by any stretch of the imagination, but he was definitely looser than normal. It had seemed like a good idea. Back in Troy's parlor, Eric had noticed how withdrawn and introspective Lorcan had been. It didn't worry Eric, but he'd love to know what was going on in his boyfriend's head when he studied him with something resembling surprise or wonder in his eyes.

"Cup of tea and toast?" Lorcan asked while walking through to the kitchen. He filled the kettle with water and turned it on.

"Sure." Eric grinned. "I can't remember the last time I had

that combination to finish a night out. Xander and I usually ended up hitting a chipper along the way home."

Lorcan put bread in the toaster and had to press the slide down three times before it stuck. Soft curses combined with cute chuckles escaped his mouth as he fought with the machine. Eric leaned against the wall and watched the show.

The evening had been simple and all the more fun for it. Very little could beat a night spent eating and drinking with good friends, and Eric wondered why people so often felt the need to push for more spectacular or unique outings. He hadn't missed the one or two absent moments Lorcan had had in the restaurant and pub, either, but when they'd vanished after he'd gotten a few more drinks in him, Eric had decided to let it go.

"Shall we have these in the living room and sit in comfort?" Lorcan turned around with a tray holding a plate with buttered toast and two mugs of tea.

Eric nodded and led the way to Lorcan's comfortable L-shaped couch. He made himself comfortable in the corner of the L and spread his legs, tapping the area between them with his hand.

Lorcan slowly lowered himself, balancing the tray until he was comfortable and able to put it on his thighs. He passed Eric a slice of toast over his shoulder and tucked into one himself. Minutes went by as they ate and drank in silence. It was another quirk of Lorcan's he really liked. Most people he knew couldn't stand quiet and always needed to be surrounded by noise, be it their own voice, music or the television, regardless of whether or not they were actually interested in what happened to be on. Lorcan, on the other hand, approached the sounds in his life the way he approached everything else — with great care. When he listened to music it was because he wanted to hear that particular piece. He only watched TV when he knew the program or movie would interest him. And he didn't do small talk.

"Let me get rid of this." Lorcan got up and took the tray back to the kitchen before returning to his spot between Eric's legs, resting his head against his boyfriend's untattooed shoulder. "So, are you sure you're not regretting your decision?"

"You mean the tattoo?" Eric considered the question for a moment. "No, I'm not regretting it at all. I thought it was a wonderful idea when you first mentioned it. I just needed to get my head around it. Are you sure you're not upset I sorta hijacked your idea?"

Lorcan turned his head and smiled at Eric. "No, I like that. I mean, I don't understand why you'd want to do that, but then, there's a lot I can't make sense of right now, so I'm trying to just go with the flow."

"You, going with the flow? Isn't that against some sort of personal rule you have?"

"Hey" — Lorcan stabbed Eric in the stomach with his elbow — "my need to think things through first isn't a rule, you know. It's just how I work." He fell silent for a moment. "But, yeah, I guess you're right. I have been acting out of character lately." He laughed. "Or rather, the way I haven't been acting lately has been out of character."

"What do you mean?" Eric spoke softly, afraid the normal volume of his voice might disturb the atmosphere between them.

Lorcan stayed quiet for a while. The edge of Lorcan's ear turned red and it was all Eric could do not to take it between his lips and caress it. He resisted the urge. Whatever Lorcan wanted to say obviously wasn't easy for him, and Eric wouldn't make it any harder than it already was, if he could help it.

"Well," Lorcan said after what felt like minutes, "you're right. I do always research everything and think things through before diving in. I want and need to know what I'm doing, what the risks are and stuff like that. But ever since you came back from Canada, things have just been happening and I've been going along as if it is the most natural thing in the world." He turned his head to glance at Eric again before settling back.

"Don't get me wrong. I'm not complaining or anything. In fact, until today I wasn't even aware it had been happening. But now that I do know…"

"You're talking about us."

"Yes, I am." Relief sounded in Lorcan's voice. "There is an us, right? I'm not imagining that?"

"You have to ask?" Eric kept his voice neutral while he wondered what on earth was going on in Lorcan's head.

"I told you. I've never been in a relationship. I honestly never thought I would be. So yeah" — Lorcan shrugged — "forgive me for being slow, but I do have to ask."

Eric wanted to ask how anybody could get to the age they both were without ever having been in a relationship. Didn't everybody in their late twenties have experience with at least one? He kept his mouth shut, sure that no matter how he phrased the question, Lorcan would hear it as either an insult or mockery.

"Turn around," Eric said instead. "I want to see your face while we have this talk."

While Lorcan stood, Eric turned onto his side, with his back against the cushions, making room for Lorcan to lie in front of him. The fact that Lorcan would be stretched out very close to the edge was a bonus, since it meant Eric had to wrap an arm around him and keep him close.

"Yes. There is an us." Eric watched Lorcan's face as joy wiped away the small frown between his eyebrows. "Didn't you hear me when I told Siobhan that you're my boyfriend?"

"Of course I did."

"But?" Eric knew there had to be more to Lorcan's answer.

"I wasn't sure whether that was you agreeing with her to keep the peace or a statement of fact."

"Statement of fact?" Eric allowed the laughter bubbling up to escape. "That's very formal."

"You know what I mean." Lorcan tried to act affronted

but the corners of his mouth moved upward. "I had no way of being sure whether or not you meant that the way it sounded? I'm forever telling half-truths when I'm visiting my parents. Or not telling them stuff at all."

Eric turned serious. "I don't lie. I even try to avoid half-truths if at all possible. You can always trust me to mean what I say and to say what I mean. Always."

"Okay." Lorcan's face lit up as a broad smile spread across it. "But..." He hesitated. "Forgive me if I'm being stupid — I'm new to this, remember — but shouldn't we talk about that, I mean, about our relationship and what we expect and stuff like that?"

For a moment, Eric's memories returned him to the time when he had been sixteen and with his first boyfriend. They'd had all those serious talks about what it meant and how they should be together. It was adorable to see a man closing in on his thirtieth birthday going through those motions for the first time. Adorable, and a privilege, he realized with a shock. He'd have to remember that some things he took for granted were new to Lorcan.

"We can talk about it, if that's what you want. We could also play it by ear and see what happens next. After all, every couple creates their own experience when it comes to relationships. I've been in a few and no two were exactly the same." Eric pushed his lips against Lorcan's before continuing. "What do you imagine this relationship of ours should be like?"

"I've no idea." Horror flashed across Lorcan's features. "First-timer, remember. Much as it may be out of character for me, I'm more than okay with floating along and seeing where we end up. I just...I don't know. Don't you have certain expectations?"

The question stopped Eric in his tracks. *Do I have expectations? Are there things I do or do not want in my relationships?* "Only two," he said when he'd made up his mind. "I expect us to be honest with each other and there'll be no cheating."

"Well, duh." Lorcan gave him a confused look. "What sort of a relationship would it be if we weren't honest? And cheating? I've never believed there are any excuses for that. If you can't be faithful to the one you're with, you shouldn't be with him." He smiled before adding, "Simples."

Eric's heart soared. If he were honest, he had to admit he didn't understand how he and Lorcan had ended up where they were any better than Lorcan did. All he knew was that it felt right. He pulled Lorcan closer and wriggled around until he was lying on his back with Lorcan on top of him. He stared into Lorcan's hazel eyes and stroked his cheek with his thumb. "That's why I love you." The words escaping his mouth took him by surprise. As true as they were, he feared they might well be too much too soon for Lorcan.

Lorcan's eyes widened before he crushed his mouth against Eric's and kissed him as if his life depended on it. "I love you, too." The words were whispered so softly that Eric had to strain to hear them, and Lorcan immediately kissing him again robbed him of the opportunity to react.

Eric tightened the hug, while also trying to free his shirt from his trousers when both of them winced and pulled back.

"Clearly I didn't think this tattoo idea through far enough." Lorcan shook his head as he pushed himself up and off the couch. He held out his hand to Eric and tugged until he stood, too. "Let's go to bed. A bit more space to play with." He smirked. "Or should I say play in? Might make things less dodgy."

"We should probably remove these bandages," Eric said after they'd both shed their clothes. "What did you do with the antibacterial cream?"

"Yeah. Damn, it's in my coat pocket. Bear with me." Lorcan dashed out of the room, leaving Eric to admire the view of his naked body. His already half-hard cock filled further at the sight of that glorious arse. He couldn't wait to get his hands on those cheeks, his mouth around that cock or for anything that might follow.

Chapter Thirteen

"Are you all right?"

Lorcan glanced at Eric and forced a smile onto his face. "Yeah. I'm fine."

Eric frowned at Lorcan then turned his attention back to the road. "I thought we'd agreed on our two rules for relationships."

Lorcan bit the inside of his cheek. Eric had a point, but the nerves swirling through his body felt so ridiculous he didn't want to share them. Maybe if he steered the conversation in a new direction...

"So, you like how your car is handling on its first drive outside the city?"

Eric made a disgusted sound before answering. "She's a pleasure to drive. Thank you for asking." He slowed down at the toll booth and handed his money over to the lad behind the glass, facing Lorcan again as he pulled away. "Now that we've got that out of the way, tell me what's wrong, please."

Lorcan knew he should have known better—Eric could be like a dog with a bone when it came to getting his way—and he sighed while he considered how to word his concerns. When his granny had first said she wanted to meet Eric, Lorcan had been delighted. Even when he'd called her back to set the date, he'd been over the moon at the thought that at least one member of his family was interested in knowing more about his life than just the bare facts. Now that they were on their way to take her out for dinner, though...

"I'm not even sure," Lorcan admitted while studiously

staring at the passing countryside rather than Eric. "I'm nervous but I can't put my finger on the exact reason. I mean, it was my gran's idea to bring you to meet her. It's not as if I'm forcing her into a potentially uncomfortable situation without her consent. Quite the opposite. But knowing that doesn't stop the nerves."

Eric stayed silent for long enough to add to Lorcan's worries and he studied his boyfriend. His gaze was fixed on the road and a slight frown had formed on his forehead.

Lorcan desperately wanted to find out what Eric was thinking but was reluctant to ask in case he wouldn't like what he heard. As he continued watching him, Eric's brow smoothed again and he smiled.

"I keep on forgetting everything we do together is a first for you," Eric said. "I know exactly what you mean. I remember the first time I brought a boyfriend home. I had no doubt he would be made welcome. I was certain my family would be their charming selves and I was a nervous wreck regardless."

"Yes," Lorcan said, relieved that he wasn't as weird as he'd thought, "that's it exactly."

Eric nodded. "You realize it shouldn't matter and yet it's important to you that she'll like me, and I her."

"Yes, that!"

"It never stops completely, I can tell you that much." Eric glanced at Lorcan and winked. "I'm glad you didn't notice, but I really wanted my family to like you, too, when we went there to collect my stuff."

Lorcan stiffened. He'd been completely unaware, probably because he'd been completely caught up in his own nerves about meeting Eric's parents and sister. Had he not paid enough attention, or was Eric simply a lot better at keeping his feelings and insecurities hidden?

"It's silly really," Eric continued. "Logically, we know it doesn't matter. My parents could have hated you and it wouldn't have changed my feelings. But then, I guess there's nothing logical about emotions."

Lorcan sagged back in his car seat as the realization hit him how far ahead Eric was of him when it came to relationships. He couldn't make up his mind whether that was a bonus or put him at a disadvantage. Should he just follow Eric's lead, sure in the knowledge he had a much better idea about what being in a relationship entailed, or should he worry about getting it so wrong that even Eric's infinite patience ran out?

Eric took one hand off the steering wheel and squeezed Lorcan's thigh. "Don't overthink it. I'm sure your granny and I will get on just fine. And as far as all the other relationship stuff is concerned, don't fool yourself into assuming I have all the answers. Just because I've been there before doesn't mean I know what I'm doing. If only because no two relationships are the same." He put his hand back where it should be. "Now, tell me where to go from here. I can't remember ever visiting Killucan."

"Just follow the road for now," Lorcan said, laughing. "I'm not surprised you're not familiar with the place. If you sneeze while driving through, you'd miss it."

Twenty minutes later Eric pulled up in front of the retirement home and Lorcan saw his granny standing outside waiting for them with a huge smile on her face.

"I knew it would be safe to wait here," she said before presenting her cheek to Lorcan for a kiss. "I can't imagine you ever being late for anything in your life." She turned and took her time looking Eric up and down. "And this is the young man you were gushing about last time I saw you?"

Lorcan was very aware of the heat erupting on his cheeks as he rushed to introduce them. "Gran, this is Eric Kavanagh. Eric, this is my gran, Mrs. Barrett."

"But Gran will do," she said while she shook the hand Eric offered and smiled up at him. "I like your taste in men." She turned to Lorcan and winked.

He felt as if he'd stepped into an alternate universe. *Who is this woman, and what has she done with the standoffish granny*

106

I've known all my life? One day he'd find the courage to ask her about that, but it probably wouldn't be today.

"Hardly young anymore," Eric said. "I'm very pleased to meet you."

Lorcan noticed how Eric avoided addressing his granny in any particular way and wasn't surprised. Calling her missus now would have been rude but using Granny within minutes after meeting the woman was probably an informality too far for him. At least, that was how it would have been for Lorcan.

"Have you decided where we're going, Gran?" Lorcan asked.

"I have. Let's go to Nanny Finn's," she giggled.

Giggled?

"Seems appropriate under the circumstances."

Lorcan vaguely remembered the place. He'd been there with his parents once or twice on past visits and if his memory served him right, the food was good. And she was right. Taking his gran to a place called 'Nanny' was just about perfect.

The restaurant was busy but not packed and they were seated within moments of arriving. The carvery was open and a short line of customers waited to be served. The smells wafting in their direction were delicious and made Lorcan's stomach rumble.

"If you tell me what you want, Gran, I'll get it for you," Lorcan said.

"I'll have a half portion of the bacon with all the sides, lad. And don't you dare pay for it. This is me treating you two to dinner." She glared at him but the sparkle in her eyes told him it was all in good fun.

"And what am I getting for you?" Lorcan turned to Eric.

"I'll come with you," he answered. "Carrying three plates on your own is asking for trouble."

When they joined the short queue Lorcan was incredibly, and not altogether comfortably, aware of Eric's presence behind him. *Fuck. It shouldn't matter.* If they'd been in

Dublin, Lorcan wouldn't even have noticed his proximity. Here, back in his home town, Lorcan couldn't shake the suspicion that all eyes were on him while people tried to work out who the man with him was and what they were to each other. He concentrated on the line moving forward as food was being served and tried to pretend he didn't feel the discomfort he resented but couldn't ignore.

"I like your granny." Eric bent forward and spoke the words straight into Lorcan's ear.

Lorcan hated himself for stiffening as Eric's breath brushed across his cheek. Turning his head to look at his boyfriend required far more courage than it should have. "I'm pretty sure she likes you, too." He forced his lips to stretch into a smile, fully aware the effort was unlikely to fool Eric.

"You're nervous again." It wasn't a question.

"Yeah. It is strange being out here. All these people know me or of me. I'll be the talk of the town for the next week or so," Lorcan said.

"You're worried about that?"

Lorcan paused for a moment before answering. "Yes and no. I mean, it doesn't make any difference to me since I don't live here anymore. And I'm sure my gran doesn't care or she wouldn't have brought us here. But word will reach my parents before the day is out and it's bound to make things even more strained between us."

Lorcan ordered the bacon dinner for his gran while he decided on beef for himself.

"I hear you," Eric said. "But that's not your fault. It's your parents who are being difficult."

While Eric waited for his dinner to be put together by the server behind the counter, Lorcan reflected that it wasn't quite as simple as that. Eric was right, of course, but past experience told Lorcan that his parents would try — and more than likely succeed — to turn it all around so that whatever embarrassment they experienced had been his fault. And he'd probably never hear the end of it.

By the time they sat back down at the table and dug into their food, Lorcan decided to push all those thoughts aside. He was here now. He'd been seen, and people would have come to whatever conclusions they wanted to draw. He couldn't control the gossip any more than he could influence the way his family would react to it, so obsessing about it was nothing more than a massive waste of time and energy.

"So," Gran said, "Lorcan tells me you're an interior designer?"

"Yes, I am," Eric responded.

"And you worked in Canada for years?"

"I did," Eric said. "But that's a thing of the past now. I don't care what happens next. I'm not leaving again."

"I think it's a crying shame the way this country continues to export our talented young people every twenty years or so. I can't remember how many times I've seen it happen during my life."

Lorcan listened to the conversation with growing wonder. How had he lived to be twenty-nine without ever knowing his gran had these views and feelings? He reversed his earlier decision not to ask any questions and turned to the grandmother who barely resembled the woman he'd grown up with. "Gran, can I ask you something?"

"Sure, lad. What's on your mind?"

"I don't mean to be rude but..." He stopped talking again, suddenly afraid this might be an intrusion too far.

"Spit it out. Come on, I won't bite." She smiled.

"You never used to be like this. For as long as I can remember you stayed out of arguments, never picking sides, no matter what was going on in our family or in the world. And now, it's almost as if I don't know you at all. You disagree with my parents, you share your opinions." He shrugged. "What happened?"

"Oh, that," she grinned. "Well, I guess you could say I've decided life's just too short to bottle everything up inside. For years, I figured it was easier not to get involved or say what I thought just to keep the peace. I didn't like arguments—in fact I still don't—but I've discovered that keeping my mouth shut is causing me far more stress than stating my opinions does. And who needs unnecessary stress in their lives?"

Lorcan nodded. "That makes sense. Thank you for telling me."

Gran wasn't finished, though. "I'm sorry it took me so long. I should have opened my mouth when your parents first started giving you a hard time and I didn't. You must have felt very alone at the time and you never really were. I've been on your side since I first suspected you might be gay. I'm sorry you didn't know."

Lorcan saw the tears appearing in his granny's eyes and covered her hand with his, squeezing softly while he swallowed hard to keep his own emotions under control.

"Don't apologize, Nan, please." Lorcan automatically reverted to the name he'd called his granny as a child. "I'm glad you told me now, and sure, if you'd said something sooner it would probably have been more hassle than it was worth."

A waiter came to clear the table and effectively put an end to the conversation before it could get any more emotional, much to Lorcan's relief. After they gave their order for tea and dessert, the conversation returned to Eric and his adventures in foreign parts. Lorcan glanced around the restaurant while listening to Eric talking about winter in Toronto. He stiffened when the door opened and a group of six adults entered. Before he fully realized what happened, his gran waved at them, effectively inviting them over, and Lorcan cursed under his breath, "Shit."

Less than a minute later Lorcan's parents, his two brothers—Rob and Christie—and Laura and her husband, Paul, had gathered around their table.

"Well, Jaysus, will ya look what the wind blew in," his father said. "To say this is a surprise would be an understatement."

Lorcan had no idea what to say and was deeply grateful his granny had no such qualms. She smiled sweetly up at her son and family while telling them to pull up chairs and join them. Lorcan watched as emotions battled on his father's face. He had no doubt the man would have preferred it if he'd been able to pretend he'd never seen them. Gran's actions had made that impossible and Lorcan also realized that his father knew as well as he did that walking away now would cause far more gossip than just sitting down ever could.

When Eric stood and held out his hand to introduce himself to the new arrivals, Lorcan's breathing stuttered. He recognized the reluctance on his mother's pinched face before she accepted the offered hand and shook it, and his father's expression wasn't any friendlier. His siblings, on the other hand, smiled broadly and appeared to be delighted with this unexpected meeting.

The subsequent conversation was painfully forced, as if all of them were dancing around subjects that couldn't be broached in polite company, and for the first time in his life, Lorcan saw his father down three whiskeys in quick succession.

"I probably shouldn't say this," his father slurred a little, "but I can't keep it to myself." He turned to face Eric. "As far as I can tell you're a decent man. And I'm prepared to accept you want nothing but the best for my son but..."

Shock was clear on Lorcan's mother's face as she silently shook her head at her husband.

"It needs to be said," he continued. "It's wrong and staying silent only makes it worse. And the idea of two men together — well I don't suppose there is polite way to say this so I'll just spit it out — it disgusts me."

"Da, I can't believe you just said that." Christie stared at his father with horror in his eyes.

"What, it's true. The whole idea..." Lorcan's father didn't finish his sentence.

"Tell me, Da." Christie leaned forward on the table,

getting as close to his father as he could without getting up. "Do you ever think about me and Emma that way?"

Lorcan held his breath as gratitude toward his brother filled him. If Christie was willing to compare him and Eric with the relationship he had with his girlfriend it had to mean he fully accepted Lorcan, didn't it?

"No! Of course not. That would just be wrong. Why do you even ask that?" The older man looked affronted.

"So, if it's not okay when it comes to me and my girlfriend, why don't the same rules apply to Lorcan?"

Silence settled over the table as Lorcan studied the faces of the people around him. His granny had a smug and proud expression on her face. He was almost sorry for the obvious embarrassment both his parents projected, while he gratefully received the encouraging smiles from his brothers and sister. He'd known he had Laura's and her husband's support, of course, but he clearly had to reassess his position in the family, if Christie's unexpected support and the expression on Rob's face were anything to go by. For the first time since he'd come out, he didn't feel like the odd one out compared to his siblings. The moment the realization struck, sympathy for his parents replaced his usual resentment. Both of them appeared shell-shocked and confused, as if their whole world had just tilted on its axis — which it probably had.

"Ma, Da." Lorcan was all too aware he had everybody's undivided attention and swallowed before continuing. "I get it, okay. I understand that it must be hard to have a son who is everything you've been taught to believe is wrong. I appreciate that you're probably worried about my soul. But this is who I am. And he" — he nodded in Eric's direction, resisting the urge to take his hand — "is the man I'm in love with. I'm not asking you to approve or like it. I just want us to get along. Surely, we're all grown up enough to put personal feelings aside and be nice to one another. It's not as if you see that much of me anyway."

"Hear, hear," Gran said while Laura, Christie and Rob

nodded.

Lorcan's dad stared at him as if he'd never seen his son before. He turned to his wife and an unspoken discussion appeared to be taking place between them. When he faced Lorcan again his features betrayed both resignation and discomfort. "I don't want this family torn apart. We've seen little enough of you in the past, son, and I've no doubt we'll see you even less if we reject your...your partner." He came very close to spitting the word out. "So yes, we can be adult about it. You and Eric" — he didn't so much as acknowledge Lorcan's boyfriend with a glance — "will be welcome in our house. But it doesn't change anything. I still think it's wrong. And I still intend to vote as the church has instructed me to vote."

Lorcan slumped in his chair. The speech had taken a lot out of him. It was as close as he'd ever come to standing up to his parents. He was grateful for the minor victory he — or rather his gran and Christie — had achieved and at the same time devastated that his parents were still as bigoted as they'd always been.

Half an hour later, as Eric drove them back to Dublin, Lorcan said as much.

"Small steps, Lorcan. Don't go looking for miracles or you're bound to set yourself up for disappointment. Give them time to get used to me. So far, your being gay has only been an idea for them. Seeing me has made it real. No matter what happens next, it will take time."

"Thank you." The words came from the bottom of Lorcan's heart. The afternoon had been an emotional rollercoaster for him and he had no idea how it had been for Eric. Right now, he didn't have the energy to ask. He needed to come to terms with all the ways in which his life and perceptions had changed first.

Chapter Fourteen

Eric opened the door to his apartment and ushered Lorcan in. His boyfriend hadn't said more than five words during their drive, clearly lost in his thoughts. Eric had kept his mouth shut, too. He wasn't sure what to say. Lorcan's situation was foreign to him. Of course, he'd heard the stories of people being rejected by their families because they were gay. He'd met quite a few men, as well as women, who had spoken about their parents with bitterness or sadness and he sympathized. He couldn't begin to imagine what it might feel like, though. He'd been shocked at Lorcan's parents' disregard for him, but it wasn't painful. They didn't mean anything to him, and while he'd prefer to be on good terms with his partner's relatives, he could live with them only tolerating him.

"Sit down. I'll get us a drink."

Lorcan nodded but still didn't speak as he all but threw himself onto the couch. Questions burned on Eric's tongue but he swallowed them while he poured two Jamesons.

"Here, get this into you." Eric held out the glass.

"Thanks." A weak smile appeared on Lorcan's face before he raised the glass to his mouth and drained it. "God, I needed that."

"Want another one?" Eric placed his own untouched glass on the table in front of them and pushed up, only to be stopped by Lorcan's hand on his arm.

"No. One will do for now."

Eric studied Lorcan and had no trouble recognizing the regret on his face.

"I'm sorry I was so withdrawn on the way home." Lorcan

lowered his gaze. "I…A lot happened this afternoon and I'm trying to make sense of it all."

"Talk to me." Eric kept his voice low, his words only a suggestion.

"I told you that when I first came out my parents told me they never wanted to meet a partner of mine."

It wasn't a question, but Eric nodded anyway.

"Even then, Laura and her husband, Paul, supported me and refused to allow my parents to use their kids as the reason why my orientation should be a big secret. And that helped—made me feel like I wasn't completely alone. Until today my brothers never said anything, just didn't get involved, I guess." Lorcan paused. "Actually, I will have another one. Stay where you are. I'll get it."

"You see"—he slowly made his way back to the couch, his eyes fixed on the glass in his hand as though it might spill, although barely a third of it was full—"if it hadn't been for Laura and Paul's easy acceptance, I would probably have walked away then. I love my family, but if every single visit was going to be a case of them against me, of me feeling utterly alone while surrounded by the very people who were supposed to love me no matter what, I would have preferred not to be there." He glanced at Eric, as if trying to determine his reaction.

"But Laura and Paul did support me. They never looked at me with suspicion when I played with their two sons. My mother did." Disgust dripped off his tongue.

Eric said nothing as Lorcan joined him on the couch again. He wanted to remark on the fact that Lorcan made sure to keep enough distance between them that none of their limbs touched, but decided against it. Lorcan was clearly working this out for himself as he spoke. He probably needed to concentrate on himself right now. Much as Eric wanted to wrap his arms around Lorcan and hold him close, it was probably not what he needed while he tried to get his head around everything he'd gone through. Later. There'd be time for comfort later.

"I mean, they were barely shocked when the abuse of young boys by priests came out and certainly never considered leaving the church, or at least viewing it with suspicion. When it came to their own son, however, they just assumed the worst."

A tiny piece of Eric's heart shattered into bits. He lifted his hand to reach out and touch Lorcan but dropped it again as Lorcan sighed.

"But, they'd promised to never turn me away and they didn't. My brothers just never talked about it in the past. With them, it was as if I'd never said anything, as if nothing had changed." Lorcan's features relaxed a little. "Until today I'd no idea whether that was good or bad. Now I know it's perfect."

Lorcan kicked off his shoes, pulled up his legs and turned to Eric, looking him in the face for the first time since they'd left the restaurant.

"I guess I'm confused."

"About what?"

"Everything?" Lorcan grimaced. "I should be over the moon to have the support of my gran, brothers and sister. And I am. But I can't get over the—I'm not even sure what to call it—rejection, reluctant acceptance, disinclination to toss aside?" He paused. "I can't help feeling that my parents would be happy to see the back of me if it weren't for the fact that it might tear the whole family asunder. And that hurts."

"Jaysus, Lorcan." Eric was lost for words. "Are you sure about that?"

"No, not sure. I am sure I disappointed them, but the rest of it could be my paranoia as easily as it could be true."

"Come here." Eric was done being patient and hands-off.

Lorcan placed his glass on the table and crawled over the couch toward Eric, who grabbed his arms and pulled until Lorcan straddled and faced him. Eric released his grip and stroked his hands over Lorcan's biceps and shoulders and up his neck until his palms rested against the stubbled cheeks.

When Eric locked his gaze on Lorcan's, he stared back without blinking for a few seconds before redirecting his attention to a spot between Eric's Adam's apple and ribcage.

"I'm sorry." Lorcan whispered the words.

"What the fuck for?" Eric only just managed to keep a handle on his frustrating helplessness.

"You shouldn't have had to sit through all that this afternoon. I hate that you had to listen to my father saying that the idea of us together disgusts him. And you shouldn't have been on receiving end of the contempt in his voice whenever he spoke about you. If I'd known how the day would go, I wouldn't have brought you." Lorcan looked up and the pain in his eyes stole Eric's breath.

"I am glad I was there." Eric spoke slowly, considering every word before he allowed it to leave his mouth. "It was an opportunity to learn more about you." He drew small circles on Lorcan's cheek with his thumb as he continued. "Don't worry about your father hurting me. The only way your parents can get to me is by hurting you." He took a deep breath while he gathered his thoughts. "I understand it's different for you, but I don't have an emotional connection to your parents. Their opinion about me wouldn't matter at all if it weren't for the fact that it matters to you. Do you know what I'm saying?"

Lorcan nodded. "Yeah. I guess I do."

"But I get what you're saying, too," Eric admitted. "It shouldn't have mattered, but I was delighted when my mother called to tell me what a charming man you were and that even Siobhan had been full of praise after we left."

A goofy grin removed all tension from Lorcan's face. "Really?"

"Yeah." Try as he might, Eric couldn't keep the pride out of his voice. "They really liked you. In fact, this is the first time my mother went to the trouble of telling me what she thought about a man I'd brought home." He pulled Lorcan closer and kissed him softly as it occurred to him that he might just have disproven his own earlier argument.

"One more thing." Eric leaned back. "And I want you to listen to me."

"One more thing and then what?" Lorcan asked, mischief glistening in his eyes.

"If you listen you'll see." Eric tried to look stern but couldn't help grinning before turning serious again.

"Don't give up on your parents just yet. I'm not saying they're going to change their minds—I don't know them well enough to be the judge of that—but until today you were sure they would never willingly meet a partner of yours. Yet there they were this afternoon, sharing a table with me, shaking my hand and being forced into acknowledging that I exist. Who's to say they won't move further once they get used to the idea?"

Lorcan smiled. "That's a great idea. From your lips and such. But for me it's going to be a case of seeing is believing. Kiss me again."

Clearly, they were done talking, and that suited Eric. He had said all he could to get his message across and now all he wanted was to make Lorcan feel good and forget about the rest of the world, miserable parents in particular. He pulled Lorcan close again and smashed their mouths together.

Eric loved the way Lorcan responded to his attack. The man who'd been passive and quiet only moments ago pushed his tongue between Eric's lips and into his mouth, giving and demanding with equal force. Eric's whole body responded. His skin was alive and his cock asserted its presence by pressing against the zip in his pants with uncomfortable insistence.

He reluctantly ended the kiss and hurriedly opened the buttons on Lorcan's shirt, releasing it from his trousers and pushing it off his shoulders as soon as he could. He stared at the tattoo. It wasn't completely healed yet—that would take a week longer at least—so Eric resisted the urge to place his hand over it and instead circled his finger around the two characters. "Never doubt your equality," he murmured. "No matter what happens, remember that you're perfect just as you are. It's not important what others say — you are as good, as strong and as much of a man as the next person."

Lorcan took his time relieving Eric of his jumper and T-shirt before copying the gesture. "Perfect, uh? When you say it I almost believe it." He raised his gaze and looked Eric straight in the eye. "I need you to fuck me. Hard."

"Not here," Eric grunted as the urgency in Lorcan's voice stoked his arousal.

Lorcan got up and held out his hand. Eric grabbed it and allowed Lorcan, who had already taken his first step backward in the direction of the bedroom, to drag him up. Lorcan released his hand again and opened the button on his trousers while walking. Recognizing a good idea when he saw it, Eric copied his movements. All he wanted was to give Lorcan exactly what he needed. If that happened to be a good hard fuck, all the better.

When they reached Eric's queen-sized bed they stopped moving long enough to shed the last of their clothing. As soon as he was naked, Eric turned Lorcan and pushed him backward so he fell on top of the covers. Eric dove after him, making sure to stop just short of crushing Lorcan. There was nothing sweet or gentle about their coming together. They lost themselves in a frenzy of hands and lips, exploring every inch of naked skin they could get in touch with. Their cocks brushed off each other and Lorcan bucked up, pressing his crotch forcefully into Eric's and rutting against him. Their mingling pre-cum turned the almost aggressive action into a slick and sensuous experience. Panting breaths filled the room, only interrupted by grunts and demands for more.

"Please." Lorcan's eyes begged as loudly as his mouth.

Eric cursed himself for having pushed Lorcan onto the center of the bed as he was forced to roll away in order to open the drawer in the bedside cabinet and grab the lube and a condom. Lorcan's impatience was infectious and Eric wasted no time, ripping the package open and sliding the protection down his hard length, fully aware of Lorcan watching his every movement. He squirted lube onto his hand and positioned himself between Lorcan's spread legs, grinning when his lover created more space for him and lifted his arse off the bed.

"Maybe you should take a leaf out of Xander's book." Eric smirked. "Patience appears to be in short supply."

Lorcan quirked an eyebrow as he lifted his head and stared pointedly at Eric's straining cock. His expression transformed into one of pure need and pleasure when Eric rubbed a lubed finger across Lorcan's taint before pressing it into his hole.

"God. Yes!" Lorcan squeezed his eyes shut. "More!"

This was a version of Lorcan that Eric hadn't encountered yet, and he marveled at the needy demanding man who appeared to be desperate for whatever Eric could give him. He didn't question it but added a second finger. He paused to give Lorcan the opportunity to adjust only to realize that his consideration was unwanted and unnecessary. Lorcan bucked against his hand, creating the friction Eric had been withholding.

"Not enough. I need more… I need you." The demand was as clear in Lorcan's voice as it was in his eyes.

Eric withdrew his hand, helped himself to more lube and stroked his cock until it was covered in the slippery substance, totally aware of Lorcan's heated attention as he did it.

Resting on his knees, he squeezed his thighs together and pulled Lorcan's arse toward him until it rested against his cock. Words had become obsolete and Lorcan raised his legs and placed his calves on Eric shoulders.

"Put your hands over your head," Eric demanded.

As soon as Lorcan complied Eric laced his fingers through his lover's, effectively pinning him to the bed. Their gazes locked onto each other as Eric pushed home. Eric wasn't sure what was sexier, the pure pleasure shining from Lorcan's eyes or the needy noises falling from his mouth.

"Now do it!"

Eric recognized an order when he received one and acted on it. He withdrew and slammed his cock home. The resulting satisfied grunt from Lorcan was deeply fulfilling. Before Lorcan could open his mouth to make further demands Eric did the same again, and again, the incoherent sounds falling from Lorcan's lips driving him on.

"Oh, God, so close."

Eric knew exactly what he meant. He wasn't far behind Lorcan. His release was building steadily, his balls drew up and a tingling sensation traveled down his spine. He tried to withdraw his right hand from Lorcan's but found himself entrapped in a steely grip.

"Do. Not. Stop." Lorcan was breathless and barely coherent.

"But…" Eric didn't have time to explain that he needed his hand to help Lorcan reach orgasm. The tension surrounding his cock increased, and he stared down his stomach at Lorcan's dick, watching in wonder as it spurted cum, untouched and unaided. The combination of sight and sensation was more than Eric could take. In a few uncoordinated pushes he shed his own release into the condom before allowing himself to collapse to the bed next to his lover.

"We really need to invest in bedside hankies," Lorcan said, his voice hoarse.

Eric chuckled softly and traced a finger through the drying wetness on Lorcan's stomach. "Best make sure they're man-sized, if this sets the standard."

Lorcan grinned as he pushed himself up and walked to the en-suite bathroom. Eric admired his man's long, slim legs and glorious arse as he moved, while taking care of the condom, grateful that he kept a small bin next to his bed. When Lorcan entered the room again, his cock almost back to its resting position and size, Eric had crawled under the covers, leaving them folded back on one side.

"Thank you. I needed that." Lorcan placed a short, sweet kiss on Eric's lips. He made sure to rest his head on the tattoo-free shoulder as he snuggled up to his boyfriend.

"Clearly," Eric whispered. "Any time."

Chapter Fifteen

"Are we right then?" Lorcan studied his friends and smiled.

Between the five of them they looked like a walking, talking rainbow. Not that the colors always matched—in fact, Eric's and Xander's shirts clashed whenever they got close to each other—but the message was loud and clear.

"I wished they'd organized this referendum for the height of summer," Eric said. "Then we could have gone bare-chested and show the tattoo off."

"Yeah. Right. Because the height of summer in this country comes with a guarantee of nice weather." Chris shook his head. "The season you call summer is a joke, mate. Winters in Sydney are warmer."

"It would have been nice, though," Lorcan said, delighted that Eric clearly felt as strongly about the tattoo as he did. He hadn't been able to rid himself of the idea that Eric had done it more for Lorcan's sake than out of conviction, and he wasn't sure if he liked that idea.

"So," Troy interjected, "what exactly are we doing today?"

"We're joining the Yes Equality bus in Tallaght. It's basically a case of handing out badges and answering questions. It should be fun." Lorcan smiled as he remembered the previous events he'd joined—sometimes alone and on other occasions with Eric. "For the last event someone brought a guitar along and spent the afternoon playing and singing."

"And no nastiness?" Xander asked.

"I haven't encountered any yet. Not while I was with the bus, anyway." Lorcan grimaced. He'd gotten some dirty looks and muttered comments on his way to and from events, though. Some people couldn't resist making snide remarks as soon as they saw the badges on his clothes. Hopefully they'd encounter less of that with the five of them traveling together.

The journey to Tallaght was entirely uneventful and the atmosphere surrounding the bus was almost carnival-like. Music came out of large speakers while a table had been set up, serving coffee and tea and showcasing a wide variety of what appeared to be home-baked treats.

"Are you sure we're canvasing?" Xander asked. "If I didn't know any better I'd say I'd walked into a street party."

"Yes and yes," Eric said. "We are canvasing. We're answering questions. We're engaging people in friendly discussion when appropriate and we're handing out Yes Equality badges and car stickers. But the party atmosphere is deliberate. We're asking people to allow us the same sort of happy ending most of them take for granted. Negativity is not going to get us anywhere, whereas fun and a positive image might persuade those in doubt that we're not dangerous extremists." He smiled, but Lorcan knew he was only half joking.

A few hours later, Lorcan turned after handing out badges to a family of six and noticed Troy talking to a man he recognized. It took him a minute before he could place the short, bald chap and in the end, it was the tattoos that clued him in on the fact it was his friend's old boss. Curious, he closed the distance between him and the men.

"Yeah." The man—Lorcan couldn't recall his name for the life of him—smirked. "He walked into the parlor two days ago, asking if I had any vacancies. He didn't tell me any details, but apparently he's back from America with no plans to leave again."

Lorcan had an idea who they were talking about and he glanced at Troy to garner his reaction.

"And will you be giving him his job back?" Troy asked.

"Yeah. I accepted him on a three-month trial basis. As far

as I'm concerned, he's starting from scratch. But from what I've seen, the Shane who came back from America isn't the same man as the one who left. I can't put my finger on it, but something has changed." He paused. "But even without that, I would have said yes. I could do with an accomplished artist for original art. And no matter what you say about Shane, he sure knows how to create magical images. I've come up against some stiff competition recently."

The look the man shot Troy before glancing at Xander held a mixture of admiration and resentment. Troy laughed. "I'll take that as a compliment." He sobered again. "You're right, Shane is good. I'm just glad he didn't ask me."

The man nodded. "I think not even Shane is brazen enough for such a move." He glanced over his shoulder. "My friends are moving on. I'd better join them. Give me a few of those badges, would you?"

Lorcan had guessed right. They had been talking about Shane—the bastard who'd talked Troy into starting a business together only to leave him stuck with it while Shane went off to America. He was proud of his friend for not holding on to all the hard feelings he must have had. It would have been so easy for Troy to spill all the beans and undermine Shane's new job before he'd even started.

"I take it that's the same Shane who caused Troy, and subsequently Xander, so much trouble a few months ago?" Eric had appeared next to Lorcan and had clearly also heard the conversation.

"Yeah. It sure sounds that way," Lorcan said. "But if it doesn't bother Troy, I'm not going to worry about it, either. Water under the bridge and such. Did you see where Chris went? This event is winding down and I'm hungry and thirsty."

"He's over there." Eric pointed to their right, where the tall Australian could be seen chatting to a group of young women. "I'll go get him."

Lorcan watched Eric as he strolled over to where Chris appeared to be having a lively discussion. He made no apologies for paying close attention to Eric's arse, beautifully framed as it was in those jeans. Not that Eric could ever be anything less than attractive, but casual wear did a lot more for him than his formal work suits ever could.

"Lorcan, have you got a moment?"

He reluctantly turned his gaze away from the view he'd been enjoying and faced the man who'd just approached him.

"Sure, what's up, Mark?" He stared at the man who was on the organizing committee of the Yes Equality bus crew.

"Didn't you say your family lives near Mullingar?"

"Yeees," he drew the word out, not sure he wanted to hear the rest of Mark's question. "They live about fifteen kilometers away, why?"

"We'll be taking the bus there next Saturday and we've been invited to take part in a public consultation that night. I'd like you to come along. It could be helpful to have a local on hand."

Every instinct in Lorcan told him to say no and be done with it. The last thing he needed was to upset his parents more than he had when he'd brought Eric to have dinner with his gran. But...did that make him a coward? Was he only able to stand up for his convictions in the relative anonymity of Dublin, or did he really stand for equality? Were his beliefs strong enough to risk alienating his father and mother? Were they worth it?

"Can I think about that for a day or so?" he asked in the end.

"Sure." Mark's face clearly showed disappointment, but he didn't push the issue. "Give me a call tomorrow and let me know."

"I will," Lorcan promised as he noticed his four friends standing together, obviously waiting for him. "Sorry, I've got to go. You'll hear from me as soon as possible." He forced a smile as he said goodbye to Mark and let it slip again as soon as the man couldn't see his face anymore.

"What was that all about?" Concern sounded in Eric's

voice, and not for the first time, Lorcan wished his expressions wouldn't betray his every thought and feeling for all to see and recognize. Knowing he'd have to tell him sooner or later, Lorcan filled Eric in, without worrying about the other three overhearing him.

"So you haven't agreed to it yet?" Troy asked before continuing when Lorcan nodded. "Yeah, I get that. It's a tricky one."

Lorcan smirked at his friend while he reflected that 'tricky one' was a gross understatement.

"I think it's simple," Chris said as they arrived at the Luas stop, joining a number of other people waiting for the tram to arrive. "I realize I'm not aware of the ins and outs of the situation, but I'd say don't do it if you don't want to."

"Would you?" Lorcan asked Troy. After all, Troy had grown up in the same area and was just as aware as Lorcan of what the attitudes had been in the past.

"I'm not sure." Troy fell silent for a moment. "Probably. But if you'd asked me a few months ago, my answer would almost certainly have been no."

The Luas arrived and nobody talked as the five of them boarded the tram. Even though their stop had been the third after the start of the line, the carriage was packed and they were forced to stand, pressed together.

"Why didn't you just say no?" Eric asked.

"Because that would be a cowardly thing to do." Lorcan allowed the thoughts to leave his mouth as they entered his head, hoping he might come up with an answer while he spoke. "I either have the courage of my convictions or I don't. And if I don't, then why am I even bothering with events like the one today?"

"You'd only be refusing to do one particular location. The bus is going all over the country. You could go to Cork or Donegal and have your say there. There's no reason why you have make a stand so close to home." Xander jumped into the discussion.

"True," Lorcan said. "That's what I'm trying to tell myself.

But it doesn't feel right. I mean, if I can't be proud of myself in front of the people who've known me since I was a little boy, the fact that I can do it anywhere else really doesn't mean much, does it?"

Silence settled while Lorcan's mind kept on spinning. When Eric grabbed his hand and squeezed, Lorcan calmed down a bit.

"See, I told you. Didn't I tell you they were queer?" The shrill voice coming from behind them and making no effort to remain unheard had the five friends staring at one another in shock.

"Shhh," somebody else giggled. "They can hear you."

"Who gives a fuck?" the painfully high voice continued at the same volume. "I mean, I don't care who does what. Each to their own, know what I mean? But, Jaysus, do they have to be so obvious about it? Holding hands in public? That's just wrong. I shouldn't have to see that, for fuck's sake."

Lorcan glanced over his shoulder and stared at the two girls sitting not a few rows behind where he stood. They appeared to be about eighteen and wore what he considered to be too much makeup. One of them had a toddler in her lap and a folded up buggy resting against the tram window.

"Stop it! He's staring at us now." The childless girl spoke while shifting her gaze to then away from Lorcan.

"So what? Let him. It's a free country. I can say what I fucking want to say. And I say that's just wrong. I don't want to have to look at two men holding hands or kissing. Eeeew, that'd be even worse."

Lorcan counted to ten in his head, hoping against hope that the other girl would have the brains to point out to her friend that in a free country he'd have as much right to hold his boyfriend's hand as she had to speak her mind. As he'd feared, no such remark was forthcoming. Instead the other girl continued.

"It's a crying shame. What a waste. They're cute. I'd do any of them in a heartbeat."

When Lorcan made a point of catching her gaze with his, he expected her to at least blush, but she just stared back at him before opening her mouth again. "I bet you I could turn them. All they need is a hot night with a good woman and that'd be the end of it."

An unexpected calm settled on Lorcan. He kept his gaze locked on the two girls as he pulled on Eric's hand until his boyfriend faced him. Bending forward, he pressed his lips against Eric's. When he pulled back someone clapped their hands behind them, soon to be joined by one or two other travelers.

"Are you okay?" Eric stared at Lorcan as if he'd never seen him before.

"I'm fine." Lorcan relaxed as a weight lifted off his shoulders. He opened his mouth to say more when he noticed the Luas was about to reach their stop. As soon as they'd disembarked he pulled his phone from his pocket and called Mark to tell him he would be going to Mullingar the following week.

"You're also going to join us for that discussion in the evening?" Mark asked.

"Yes. I'll be there, too. Sorry to have kept you hanging."

"No worries, mate." Mark laughed. "I'm just glad you got there in the end."

"Yeah, that makes two of us," Lorcan muttered as he ended the call. He stared at his screen for a moment before putting his phone away, raising his gaze and finding his four friends scrutinizing him. "What?"

"Are you sure about that?" Eric studied him. "Why didn't you wait until tomorrow before calling him back? Are you certain you've made up your mind?"

Lorcan shrugged. "It wasn't so much me making up my mind as those girls making it up for me. There's so much ignorance and fear out there when it comes to LGBT issues. If people like us — me — refuse to speak up, how are we ever going to end that?"

"Good point," Troy said. "But the fact remains that you'll

be going to a meeting where you're bound to meet people you know. Priests, former teachers, family members. There's a difference between confronting the world and going up against people you've known all your life."

For a moment doubt assailed Lorcan. Had he been too hasty? Should he just have said no, or at least thought about the issue longer before making up his mind? He turned to Eric, found him thoughtfully studying him and was instantly certain he hadn't made a mistake. Their relationship was worth standing up for. His truth had as much right to be heard as anybody else's. He was as entitled to be loved and have that love acknowledged as any other person. He wasn't going to hide anymore.

Eric's face relaxed and his eyes sparkled. "Yes, he's made up his mind all right," he answered Troy's question. "And he won't be alone."

"I won't be?" Lorcan tilted his head. "You don't have to come with me."

"I'm aware of that," Eric said, "but I want to."

Although he'd meant it when he said Eric didn't have to join him in Mullingar, Lorcan couldn't help feeling relieved that he wouldn't have to face that no doubt stressful event on his own.

"I wish we could come, too," Troy sounded troubled. "But I can't change the plans we have for next Saturday. I'm sorry."

"Don't worry about it." Lorcan shrugged. "I'm sure it will be fine." He knew no such thing, but he was certain that whatever happened next weekend, he'd feel better for having faced it than he would have if he'd allowed his fear to keep him away.

"Now, how about some of that food and drink we were talking about earlier?"

Chapter Sixteen

Eric blinked at the suddenly blurry screen of his computer as the fourth coming-out video he'd been watching ended. He stared at the suggested other stories he could watch, impressed with the sheer number of vlogs available. As far as he could tell, most if not all had been uploaded over the past few months, more than likely as a reaction to the referendum. He smiled when he realized that the vote Yes campaign had probably given them the courage to do so. No matter whether or not the referendum passed, a lot of gay people in Ireland felt more secure now than they had in the past.

He'd always known how lucky he was. His parents hadn't blinked an eyelid when he'd told them he was gay. In fact, they hadn't even appeared to be surprised. What he'd never realized was just how exceptional their behavior had been. Sure, he'd heard and read the stories about kids being kicked out of their parental homes after coming out. He'd been horrified when he'd first found out about conversion therapies and the fact that people actually subjected their children to torture like that. Until recently it had been an abstract knowledge, though, something he knew existed but couldn't really imagine.

He sighed as he checked the time and realized Lorcan should be home shortly. Lorcan. Meeting his boyfriend's parents had brought the theoretical into the real world for Eric. It broke his heart to think that Lorcan's parents had distanced themselves from one of their children as soon as they had realized he wasn't able to be the God-fearing, grandchild-producing son they'd always assumed he would be. The real fear these kids in the videos had experienced before coming out to their own loved ones had only reinforced Eric's sympathy for Lorcan. His boyfriend had never said it in so many words, but Eric had no problem imagining how devastating it must have been when the people who'd raised him, who were supposed to love him unconditionally, had turned away from him because he didn't meet their expectations. His finger hovered over his mouse, ready to start the next video, when he heard the key turn in his front door.

"God, what a day," Lorcan grumbled by way of hello.

"Had a tough one?" Eric got up from his desk and walked to where Lorcan was taking off his coat. He drew his boyfriend close for a warm and lingering kiss as soon as his arms were free again.

"Hmmmm," Lorcan murmured, the motion of his lips teasing Eric's. "Tell you about it in a minute. Give me another kiss."

Eric was only too happy to oblige and pressed his lips more firmly against Lorcan's welcoming mouth, deepening the kiss as he went. When they pulled apart again, their breathing louder than it had been, Lorcan's face had relaxed into a lazy and somewhat heated smile.

"So, what happened in work today?" Eric asked.

The frown instantly reappeared on Lorcan's face and Eric lifted his hand to smooth a finger over it and brush it away again.

"I had to sit in on a meeting with a client today. Once the official part was over he started talking about the referendum and how disgusting the whole idea of two men marrying was to him." Lorcan smirked. "It's funny how he didn't seem to have an issue with two women striking up a relationship." He turned away from Eric and walked to the kitchen. "I need a beer. Want one?"

Eric nodded and waited for Lorcan to return and finish his story. He had an inkling there was more to come.

"Anyway," Lorcan said after he'd settled himself on the

couch next to Eric. "I know my boss is in the Yes camp. He's told me so from the start, but it hurt that he would just let the man spout all his bigoted hatred without objecting even once. And, of course, I couldn't say anything." Bitterness crept into Lorcan's voice. "As soon as the potential client started on the subject, my boss threw me a warning glance. I was this close" — he indicated a width of about two centimeters with his fingers — "to opening my mouth anyway." Lorcan shrugged. "But I can't afford to lose my job. And if I am the reason the company doesn't get certain clients, I won't be there much longer. So I swallowed my anger, but it was hard."

"I'm sure it was," Eric said as he tugged Lorcan closer and stroked his back.

"Mind you" — Lorcan sounded more relaxed — "I bet my boss was very glad I'd come to the meeting without my jacket on. The Yes badge is there for the duration and I wouldn't have taken it off, regardless of the client's opinion or my boss' wishes."

Eric chuckled. "Isn't it a shame you didn't have an opportunity to bring that client into your office. He would have gotten the message without you having to say a word."

"But I did, right before we went..." Lorcan threw back his head and laughed. "That's it. I was wondering what possessed the man to go into a full-on attack on the referendum when it had nothing to do with the business we'd been discussing. Now I get it. He accompanied me to my desk when I had to get my paperwork. He must have noticed the badge then. Best not share that bit of information with my boss." He sniggered before turning his head and engaging Eric in a long, deep kiss.

"What were you doing when I walked in?" Lorcan asked, nodding in the direction of the still open laptop. "Were you working? Did I interrupt you?"

"What?" Eric glanced at the now black screen on his computer and shook his head. "No, I was watching some videos about kids taking advantage of the referendum and coming out to their families. It's amazing how many of those you can find. I'm not sure I'd ever record something like that. I mean, even with my parents probably being the easiest people in the world, I still can't imagine putting such a private moment on for public display."

"Are they all happy videos?" Lorcan asked.

"So far, they have been," Eric responded. "Mind you, that may well be the result of the way I'm selecting them. I mean, I just allow one episode to direct me to the next. I'm sure there's some sort of algorithm ensuring what I see is more of the same rather than the exact opposite."

"Yeah. I guess." Lorcan sounded distracted. "I think I might like to see a few of those, but I need to eat something first. What do we have?"

As they prepared dinner together — Lorcan in charge of the pasta and Eric taking care of the salad and garlic bread to accompany it — Eric wondered whether he should have mentioned the videos he'd been watching and if it wasn't a bad idea for Lorcan to watch them. Wouldn't every positive reaction just reinforce the pain of his own parents' rejection? He wanted to ask the question but couldn't make himself do it, convinced that mentioning it would potentially be as painful as seeing the happy footage might be.

"I've got some news, too," Eric said once they sat down to eat. "And I'm not sure whether it's good or bad."

"Go on," Lorcan said after he'd swallowed the food in his mouth.

"Carmel and I got notice from our landlord today. The renewal date for the lease is coming up and he's decided to double our rent." The anger Eric had experienced when he'd first read the letter bubbled up inside him again. "It's ludicrous. He was overcharging us to begin with. This just takes the rent to ridiculous levels. But he must think he can find a tenant willing to pay that sorta money." He took a bite of his garlic bread before continuing. "It won't be us, though. Business may be picking up, but it's nowhere near good enough to cover the amount he's suggesting."

"Shit." Lorcan stopped eating and stared at Eric, clearly horrified. "What are you two going to do? You won't have to go abroad again, will you?"

"Fuck no," Eric exclaimed. "That was Carmel's first suggestion. She figures that if we accept more foreign assignments we might just be able to swing it. I told her I have no intention of leaving again. If that's how she wants to play it, she can do the traveling."

"And?"

Eric knew the smile on his face had to be tinged with bitterness. "She has no intention of going anywhere. I mean, she couldn't possibly be expected to leave Dublin and her family and friends behind, now could she? Whereas she doesn't think twice about insisting it's exactly what I should do."

"So, what will you do?" Lorcan asked.

"We have two months to come up with a solution. We've written to the leasing company informing them we've no intention of signing the new lease, which means we'll have to be out by the end of June." Eric tried to sound lighthearted about it all. This was his problem, so there was no need to worry Lorcan. "We have options. We'll be searching for cheaper, yet still presentable offices. If that doesn't work out we may end up having to go our separate ways and try to find a position within another, more established design company."

"Would you want to do that?"

"Fuck no!" Eric pushed his chair away from the table, gathered their now empty plates and took them over to the sink. He continued talking with his back to Lorcan as he rinsed them before placing them in the dishwasher. "I like being self-employed, doing my designs exactly the way I see them in my mind. Working for others means I lose a lot of the freedom I have now." He turned to the table where Lorcan still sat, staring at him, and shrugged. "But needs must and all of that shit." He forced a smile. "Enough about that for now. There's nothing we can do about it tonight and I do have some time to come up with a solution. Let's watch a few of those videos, if you're still interested."

They brought the laptop from Eric's desk to the couch and settled in, the device on Lorcan's lap so he'd have the best view.

"I already saw most of these," Eric said when Lorcan pointed out that he would have to watch at an angle. "There, start with that one. It's rather sweet."

Instead of turning to the screen, Eric studied Lorcan as he watched the recordings. After all, he had seen them before and the mixture of emotions passing over his boyfriend's face told him so much about the man he'd fallen for…hard. Lorcan smiled when the parents in question came up with exactly the right reaction to their child's revelation, and Eric's heartbeat stuttered as Lorcan frantically blinked when one of those youngsters explained how wonderful it had been to have received their parent's unconditional support. He tried to imagine what Lorcan might be thinking, and wondered if he was envious. Did watching these videos make Lorcan feel better or worse? He didn't open his mouth to ask, though. If Lorcan wanted to tell Eric, he would.

After the fifth video Lorcan didn't click on a new link but sat back and turned to Eric. "This is all well and good, but it's rather one-sided. Of course, these are all happy stories. Would you post what you'd recorded if it had all gone horribly wrong?"

"Oh, but they do." Eric turned the laptop so he had easy access to the keyboard and typed in a few words until the search engine came up with an article he'd read earlier. "Are you sure you want to see this? I mean, this is not a happy tale. Not at all."

"Yes." Lorcan's reply was instant and sure. "I want a realistic mix of what's happening. Not just the happy stories."

Eric figured it made sense, clicked on the link and turned the screen back to Lorcan. Anger darkened Lorcan's handsome features as soon as he'd read the first few words.

When he activated the sound file, Eric held his breath, fully aware of what was coming next and worried about Lorcan's reaction to it.

Lorcan squeezed the hand resting on Eric's thigh into a fist as the sounds of abuse and things being thrown burst from the laptop. Curses and shouting alternated with a soft voice pleading for understanding, and Eric could only be grateful there were no images to go with the sounds as Lorcan's breathing got shorter, as if he'd just run a long distance. Eric wanted to kick himself for not having stopped his boyfriend from watching this.

"Jaysus fucking Christ," Lorcan whispered when the recording finished with the young man in question being kicked out of the house where he'd grown up. "That kid's still in school. How can parents do that? I mean, to their own kid? What's wrong with them?" Lorcan shoved the laptop at Eric, twisted, pulled his wallet from his back pocket and reclaimed the laptop.

"What are you doing?" Eric asked as Lorcan clicked on a link at the bottom of the page and started typing.

"Sponsoring him. Look, they've set up a page for him." He pointed at the screen. "And people have already been giving money," Lorcan sounded a bit less angry. "If enough of us do that he may not end up homeless and on the street." He extracted his credit card and entered the details before hitting the submit button. "I never thought I'd be grateful for the parents I have, but I guess this puts it all in perspective." He stared at Eric and the emotion in Lorcan's eyes made Eric hurt inside. "Just goes to show that there's always somebody out there who's got it even worse."

"At least that was in America," Eric said in the hope it would alleviate the pain Lorcan was so clearly feeling.

"Doesn't mean it doesn't happen here, too," Lorcan growled. "Have you seen all the youngsters sleeping rough? I bet you at least a few of them are on the street because something like this happened to them." He fell silent and gazed off, past Eric, as if he wasn't there.

"You see," Lorcan continued after a few minutes, "that's another reason the referendum is so important. Not because those kids may want to marry one day, although it would be nice if they could, but because it will be another step toward normalizing what is still seen as strange and objectionable." He stopped talking again before whispering, "That's what makes it really important. That's what scares me."

"Why does it scare you?" Eric surprised himself by also lowering his voice.

"Because if we don't win, it will mean so much more than not being able to get married. It will be the rejection of a large part of the population by the majority. It will be a statement to those kids that they really aren't good enough. And the No campaigners are so loud, and so very good at scaremongering, I'm not sure our message is coming across. It would be funny if it wasn't so scary." Lorcan laughed but it wasn't a happy sound. "If we're depending on people like me to convince people to vote in favor of the referendum, what chance do we have?"

"Hey." Eric fully turned to Lorcan and took his face in his hands, forcing Lorcan to meet his gaze. "Don't put yourself down like that. You're clever, you're articulate and you're far more reasonable than those others could ever hope to be."

"Thank you." Lorcan's attempt at a smile was feeble at best. "But that's not what I mean. I'm not putting myself down. But I'm also no professional or trained public speaker, and those naysayers almost invariably are."

Eric knew Lorcan was thinking about Mullingar and more than likely having to get up and address a mostly hostile crowd. The meeting wouldn't take place for another three days, though, and Eric figured it wouldn't do Lorcan any good to obsess about it for all that time.

"Let's watch something else. I saw an Irish video today you might like. This one is all upbeat and optimistic." Eric found the link and clicked on it before turning to watch Lorcan again. If Lorcan's reaction was anything like his had been earlier, Eric had no doubt he'd have his happy Lorcan back in a few short minutes.

Lorcan's face changed as the political ad showed people gathering to go to the voting stations for the referendum. Parents went with kids, grandparents were picked up and brought along, the message loud and clear — families should unite to say Yes to love. Eric smiled again, only for his joy to evaporate when he realized Lorcan looked increasingly unhappy as the video continued.

"What a load of bollix!" Despite having seen the warning signs, Lorcan's outburst took Eric by surprise.

"What do you mean? I think it's a wonderful ad. Especially the bit about the man worrying about how his father might vote and the happy ending outside the polling station."

"That's exactly what I meant. Pure shite. That's fiction. Do you really believe that happens in real life? The reality of it is that people who won't commit to a Yes vote by now will almost certainly reject the referendum on the day. Take my parents. The chance of them changing their minds and suddenly voting Yes are nonexistent." Lorcan spat out the words. "They've made that abundantly clear."

Bollix. That was the one angle Eric hadn't considered before showing the ad. "But you don't know that for sure. They could change their minds." Even as he said the words, Eric had to admit to himself that it was an unlikely scenario.

"Yeah, I guess." Lorcan deflated as anger appeared to be replaced by resignation. "And pigs might fly." He swallowed. "I'm sorry. I didn't mean to take it out on you. None of this is your fault. I just get so bloody frustrated."

Eric picked up the laptop and returned it to its usual place on his desk before walking back to the couch. He held out his hand and pulled Lorcan up when he grabbed it. "Let's go to bed. I can think of one or two ways to take your mind off matters referendum-related." He smirked and breathed a sigh of relief when Lorcan grinned back at him.

Chapter Seventeen

Lorcan walked out of his job without any of the relief Friday evenings normally brought. Any other weekend, he'd be looking forward to relaxing, maybe a night out and spending quality time with Eric. He sighed when he thought about his boyfriend. He wouldn't have blamed Eric if he was totally exasperated with him. He'd been moody and argumentative ever since Wednesday, and with the weekend and the dreaded meeting in Mullingar coming closer with every passing day, his mood swings had only gotten worse.

As he loosened his tie he wondered, not for the first time, if he should talk to Eric about everything that had been going through his mind ever since he'd said yes to traveling to the Midlands. Eric probably deserved to be told why he'd been acting like a little shit at times. On the other hand, however, did he really have the right to burden his boyfriend of just a few months with all the turmoil he experienced? Would that be fair?

He stopped at a pedestrian light and watched the rush-hour traffic snake its way past him — slowly and bumper to bumper. He wished he had a better idea about how relationships were supposed to work. How much of himself was he supposed to share? How much did he want to tell Eric? He was used to figuring things out for himself and not at all convinced having a second opinion thrown in would help him find the answers he so sorely needed. Should he just ask Eric what the man expected? But if he did, wouldn't that make him look like an incredible loser, not to mention a dumb one?

The questions circled through his head as he walked toward the pub where he would be meeting Troy, Xander and Eric. With a bit of luck, an evening spent with his friends would take his mind off the nerves gathering in his stomach. A few pints more than he usually drank might help as well.

Friends. It was funny how he'd never had any doubts about discussing his problems with Troy. But then he'd known Troy almost all his life. He usually knew what Troy would say before he even opened his mouth. Talking to Eric was—or at least felt—different. He was fairly sure Eric really cared about him, but would that last if he revealed how scared he was? Nobody liked a coward, or a moaner for that matter. For the first time since he'd started on that train of thought, a smile tugged at his lips. *I guess that really depends on the circumstances preceding the moaning.*

He tried to force his mind in a different direction, but the closer he got to his destination the more pressing the question became as to whether or not he should tell Eric what was bothering him. For the first time since they'd gotten together, he wished he had previous experience with relationships. The only example he had to go by was the way his parents conducted their marriage, and he couldn't help feeling the friendly but distant atmosphere between them wasn't something he should be aiming to replicate. He played with the idea of asking Troy for advice before dismissing it again. Not tonight, anyway. This evening would be all about relaxing and hopefully forgetting, for a few hours at least, about what he would have to face tomorrow. A public speech in front of a more than likely unsympathetic audience. Mark had called him to confirm that he almost certainly would be asked to address the crowd and his stomach cramped as he wondered why he had ever imagined agreeing to make that journey might be a good idea.

No! As he approached the meeting place he made up his mind. He wouldn't talk to Eric. It wouldn't be fair to worry him, or make him feel as if he had to come up with solutions for what wasn't his problem. Lorcan was a grown man, and as such he should be able to figure this out for himself and deal with it. He pushed open the door to the lounge area of the pub with a sigh of relief. Inside he would hopefully find the distraction he needed.

"Can you believe two weeks from today we will all have voted?" Troy asked when he returned from the bar, carrying a tray of pints.

Lorcan sighed. Hoping the referendum wouldn't come up tonight had probably not been realistic on his part. Eric squeezed his thigh and he turned to his right to find his boyfriend staring at him, one eyebrow raised questioningly. Lorcan wordlessly shook his head in reply and smiled, knowing only too well that Eric could read him like a book and never fell for the fake expressions Lorcan produced. Sure enough, Eric frowned before redirecting his attention to the conversation between Xander and Troy.

"All the polls are predicting a clear victory for the Yes vote," Xander said. "I'm not sure what everybody is so worried about. Seems to me we've got this one in the bag."

"I won't believe it until the result has been announced," Eric said, expressing Lorcan's thoughts accurately. "It has happened too often in the past. All the forecasts predict a certain result and then some people decide there's no need for them to make the effort and actually vote because it's a done deal anyway. Or it rains and people can't be bothered to leave their houses because they don't want to get wet."

Lorcan's mood was rapidly going down the drain and still he couldn't stop himself from adding his two cents. "The outcome of this referendum has no consequences for most of the people eligible to vote. That's what I worry about. I mean, why should they bother coming out to vote on something that won't change their life one way or another?"

"Nah, I don't buy that." Troy stared at him with concern in his eyes and Lorcan winced. It was bad enough he couldn't keep his mood and worries concealed from Eric, and he didn't need Troy in on the act, too. "I'd say that virtually everybody in this country knows at least one person who is gay. If they're not voting for themselves, they'll probably vote for their friends or kids. I mean" — Troy grinned — "I would."

"I hope you're right," Lorcan said while scrambling to come up with something else to talk about.

"On a completely different note…" Troy grinned at his boyfriend before looking at Eric and Lorcan. "Xander has persuaded me to make him a partner in the shop."

"Really?" Eric asked. "That's huge."

"Not really." Xander smiled self-consciously. "I mean, nothing much is going to change. Troy will still be in charge of the shop and I still won't know the first thing about tattooing, but it takes care of Troy's continued discomfort about the designs I create and refuse to take payment for."

"It so is huge," Troy objected. "I mean, I stopped worrying about the shop surviving a while ago and business is good enough that I can afford to pay Chris' wages without lying awake about it at night. But once Xander actually owns half the place we can think about modernizing, maybe even expanding in a few years." Troy drank deeply from his pint before continuing. "I'm serious. It's a huge weight off my shoulders. Running a business on your own means you carry all the risk and stress as well. Having a boyfriend like Xander who will listen when I need to moan helps, of course, but now we will truly share the responsibility."

Lorcan stared at his friend and realized he did look far more relaxed than he ever had since he'd first opened his shop. He could have kicked himself. He'd been so caught up in his own worries he'd been paying no attention to the people around him. Troy was supposed to be his best friend. He'd known him for years. He should have noticed something had changed.

"Anybody for another drink?" They all nodded and Xander got up to get them, Troy coming along to give him a hand.

"Are you okay?" Troy and Xander hadn't disappeared from earshot before Eric turned to Lorcan and asked his question.

"Yeah, I'm fine." Lorcan waved his hand through the air. "Just a lot on my mind, that's all."

"If there's anything I can do," Eric said, concern shining in his eyes. "You know you only have to ask. Right?"

Lorcan sighed. The chances of Eric dropping the issue were slim to none. "Yes, thanks. And I appreciate it. It's one of those things I just need to get my head around and I'll be fine again. Don't worry about it. Let's just enjoy the evening."

Eric looked unconvinced to say the least, but since Troy and Xander picked that moment to return with the drinks he just nodded and dropped the subject, much to Lorcan's relief.

The rest of the evening ran as smoothly as Lorcan could have wished for. None of the subjects they talked about were heavy or loaded, jokes flew around the table, with each of them being on the receiving end of one at least once, and drinks went down smoothly. By the time midnight came around and they decided to call it a night, Lorcan dared to hope he'd gotten his wish after all.

"You're off to Mullingar tomorrow, aren't you?"

They were standing outside in front of the pub when Troy asked his question and shattered Lorcan's illusion.

"Yes, I am." Lorcan repressed a heavy sigh.

"I'm still sorry we can't make it," Troy said.

"Don't worry about it." Lorcan smiled at his friend while meaning the words as he said them. The smaller his audience would turn out to be, the better, as far as he was concerned. "Tomorrow is a Saturday, probably the busiest day of the week for you. Of course you can't come along."

"Hmmm," Troy grumbled. "I still feel I should be there. It's my hometown, too. I should be helping."

"Eric is coming with me," Lorcan said, although he was no longer sure whether or not that was a good thing. "I'm sure he'll hold my hand should I need it." He laughed, but even to his own ears it sounded forced, and Troy didn't look convinced.

"Okay, just let me know how you got on when it's all over." Troy reached for Lorcan and pulled him close in a hug. "You've got this," he whispered in Lorcan's ear before releasing him again.

Lorcan stared at Xander's and Troy's backs as they strolled away and believed Troy's words until his friends turned a corner and disappeared from sight.

"Shall we?" Eric asked, a cautious note in his voice.

"Sure." Lorcan turned and glanced at Eric as he took his first step on the short walk home. As he had feared, Eric studied him with concern etched on his face. All the more reason to keep his mouth shut. If Eric was worried about him now, he'd only make matters worse if he unloaded all his stress on him, too. Another twenty-four hours and, for better or for worse, the whole ordeal would be behind them.

They made their way in silence until they turned into their street.

"What I don't understand," Eric said suddenly, "is why you won't tell me what's bothering you. You've been growing ever more distant over the past few days and yet you pretend nothing is wrong. Is it this trip to Mullingar or is something else bothering you?"

"It's nothing!" Lorcan regretted allowing himself to snap the moment it happened but couldn't stop it. "Can't I just be in a lousy mood every now and again? I mean, I'm only human. I'm not going to be Mister Happy every day of the week."

"Whoa, hold on a minute." They'd reached the front door of their building and Eric used his key to open it. "I only asked the question because something appears to be eating you. No need to bite my head off because I'm concerned."

Lorcan felt like a heel but between the nerves churning in his stomach and his decision not to burden Eric with everything going on in his mind, he couldn't deal with Eric going all mother hen on him, too. He'd been taking care of himself for over ten years quite successfully and didn't need somebody else to take charge of his life now. He took a deep breath and tried for a more reasonable tone.

"I'm sorry. That was a bit over the top." He couldn't bring himself to look at Eric, knowing full well that his boyfriend would realize things were far from fine as soon as he caught a glimpse of Lorcan's face. "It's just—I don't know—life." Keeping it vague was definitely the best option right now.

They stopped walking as they reached the point on their landing where they usually decided whether they'd go left into Lorcan's apartment or right into Eric's.

"I don't buy it." Eric sounded stubborn. "Something is upsetting you and I'd feel a lot better if you'd just tell me what it was." He paused for a moment before adding, "Where do you want to sleep tonight?"

Something short-circuited inside Lorcan. "Maybe I don't want to tell you what's up. Has that occurred to you?" Because he forcibly kept himself from shouting, his voice sounded far more menacing than it should have. "Can't you just leave it be? I'll be over it soon enough. Your badgering is only making me feel worse." He still refused to meet Eric's gaze, afraid of the pain and confusion he would almost certainly find written on his face, and stared at his own door instead. "You know what? I think I'd rather be on my own tonight. I'll see you tomorrow. We'll need to leave at about eleven. That is if you're still coming with me." Without waiting for a reply, he turned, unlocked his door and opened it.

"Of course I'm still going with you. Lorcan, don't—"

He had no way of knowing what Eric said next because he shut the door behind him as soon as he stepped over the threshold. He had a pretty good idea what the rest of the sentence would have been, though. *I'm such a prick.* Eric didn't deserve to be treated like this. He turned and had his hand on the door handle, ready to cross the landing and apologize, when he stopped himself. If he went to Eric now he'd stay the night and Eric would, without a doubt, want to talk about what'd just happened and what was bothering Lorcan. He had enough self-awareness to realize he'd lash out even worse if that happened. He'd end up saying things he wouldn't be able to take back.

He walked straight to his bedroom and shed his clothes as soon as he was inside. Lorcan knew he probably needed a shower but he couldn't be bothered. Tomorrow morning would do. He crawled under the covers and made himself as small as possible in the middle of the bed that seemed far too big now that he had it to himself for the first time in months. Fervently hoping he'd had enough to drink to lull him into sleep, Lorcan closed his eyes.

Chapter Eighteen

Eric studied Lorcan as he drove them along the N4 to the Midlands and couldn't help worrying. His hands were squeezing the steering wheel just a bit too tightly. Lorcan's features appeared frozen in something between determination and surrender. Several times he'd opened his mouth to suggest going back to Dublin, only to press his lips together and keep the words inside. Lorcan had made up his mind to do this. And regardless of whether it would turn out to be a good decision or one fraught with painful consequences, it had been Lorcan's to make. Therefore, abandoning the idea would have to be up to him as well. That didn't mean Eric had to like what it was doing to his boyfriend right now.

My boyfriend. Eric grimaced. Was that still the case? What the fuck had happened last night? He'd spent long and sleepless hours trying to figure it out but answers had been elusive.

Lorcan had been almost euphoric, the first few days after they'd come back from the rally in Tallaght, as if he'd shed a colossal weight from his back. He'd been optimistic and using Eric as a sounding board as he figured out what he might say during the meeting they were to attend. The enthusiasm had started to wither on Wednesday, after they'd watched the videos. Eric still didn't understand what had happened there. He'd expected those stories might inspire Lorcan but they'd achieved the exact opposite.

Lorcan's refusal to talk to him, combined with his announcement that he wanted to spend the night on his own, had been like a punch in the gut, but he'd bitten his tongue and gone to his own bed, in his own apartment... alone. Not that he'd had much of a choice after Lorcan had shut his front door in his face, but he'd refrained from texting and calling, no matter how hard it had been. Waking up without Lorcan beside him this morning had been a strange and, if he were honest, unpleasant experience. He'd only spent a few nights apart from Lorcan since coming back from Canada and clearly Lorcan had become part of Eric's normal, in the two short months since his return.

"Did you tell anybody you're going to be in Mullingar today?" Eric couldn't stand the silence anymore. Just because he didn't want to talk about their relationship until they'd put the public discussion behind them didn't mean he had to keep his mouth shut all day. Maybe if Lorcan hadn't vetoed having the radio on, his uncommunicativeness might have been bearable. Under the circumstances, it drove Eric up the wall.

"Just my gran." Lorcan didn't take his eyes off the road for even a split second and the knuckles on his hand were slowly turning white. "She would have never let me hear the end of it if she'd discovered I'd been in town without letting her know."

"Will she be there?" Eric asked, although Lorcan's gran was very low on his list of things he wanted to talk about right now.

For the first time in ages, Lorcan's features relaxed and a small smile appeared on his face.

"If we were talking about anybody else I'd say no. I mean, she doesn't have her own transportation, and who is she going to ask to drive her to the venue? But my gran has always done everything her own way, so I wouldn't be surprised if she showed up."

Eric stared out of the window at the fields as they appeared to be flying by. "Would you be okay with her being there?"

Lorcan laughed, although it was anything but a happy sound. "She's about the only person I won't mind seeing. If everybody besides her and you turns out to be a complete stranger, I'll be a very happy man."

Eric sighed as he once again swallowed the suggestion to turn the car around and go home. Unhappy as he was, Lorcan was clearly also determined to see this through, and Eric wouldn't be the one to undermine him. He just wished Lorcan would talk to him. They hadn't had any issues communicating before. Now that Lorcan had decided to shut up shop and keep his thoughts and feelings to himself, Eric had no idea how to deal with it. Should he push? Pretend it wasn't happening? Should he be worried? Had he somehow missed the moment Lorcan had decided he didn't want to be in a relationship anymore? The questions burned on his lips but he didn't vocalize them. He'd give Lorcan the benefit of the doubt until the Mullingar meeting was behind them. But, Jaysus, just the idea that Lorcan might well be about to end things between them made Eric nauseated.

Lorcan turned on the indicator and moved onto the exit ramp. At least they were nearly there. The car was too small and claustrophobic for the two of them right now. After he'd parked fifteen minutes later, Lorcan stared at him over the roof of the car and Eric thought he might be about to say something, but Lorcan averted his gaze, turned and walked away without a word. *What the fuck?*

Half an hour after they'd joined the Equality bus and crew, Lorcan seemed to relax. He talked with passersby and joked with the other campaigners, Eric included. But Eric knew he wasn't imagining the stress bubbling just beneath the surface in Lorcan.

The afternoon passed slower than Eric would have liked. When he caught himself checking his phone screen for the tenth time in an hour he admitted defeat and conceded he wouldn't be able to relax until he had Lorcan to himself again, and could at last get answers to the questions he should have posed while they'd been driving here. As much as Lorcan not telling him what was going through his mind upset Eric, he couldn't deny that he had a responsibility, too. If he wanted answers he should ask the questions.

"There you are, my boy."

Despite the worries churning through his stomach, Eric couldn't help smiling when Lorcan's granny made straight for her grandson and pulled him in for a kiss and a hug. The fact that she was being followed by at least another ten elderly people only made him smile wider.

"I hope you brought enough badges, lad. All my friends" — Lorcan's gran waved to indicate the people clustered around her — "want one, and a few to spare to give to their families. Don't you?" She all but glared at the group, and Eric would have been impressed if any of them had been brave enough to deny her. None were, and Eric had to admit they all appeared genuinely happy to don the badges.

"We're also going to that meeting tonight." The older lady smiled. "We need to show those naysayers that they can't have it all their own way."

The smile faded from Lorcan's face as soon as his granny mentioned the meeting.

"There's no need for you to come, Gran. It's not as if we have to convince you," Lorcan all but pleaded with her.

"Nonsense, of course I'll be there. Besides, the taxi to bring us back won't be here till ten o'clock tonight. What else are we going to do? There's not even a bingo game happening anywhere."

Lorcan threw back his head and laughed, resembling the man Eric had come to know and — if he were honest — take for granted, for the first time in four days. Eric couldn't help joining in. Bingo games and the Irish obsession with them would never fail to bemuse him.

"Are you boys nearly done here?" She turned from Lorcan to Eric and back again. "We'd like you two to join us for a bit of dinner. The meeting won't start for another few hours."

Lorcan glanced at Eric, who just shrugged, before telling

his gran they'd be delighted to join them, while Eric reflected how much easier that would be than having to eat with just Lorcan, while he was his silent and brooding self.

Two hours later, as they walked through the door of the community hall where the marriage equality discussion was to take place, all the tension Lorcan had shed during their meal rushed back, if the way he hunched his shoulders and the frown on his forehead were anything to go by. They claimed chairs on the front row, Lorcan stiff as a plank and staring straight ahead while Eric turned to the back to keep an eye on people entering the venue. He nearly nudged Lorcan when he thought he recognized Lorcan's parents but stopped himself. Considering how tense Lorcan already was, knowing his father and mother were here probably wouldn't help.

After over an hour of listening to all the reasons people should vote No, Eric wanted to scream. They were the same claims he heard on radio and television every day, and they didn't get any less ridiculous just because people kept repeating them.

"Thank you, ladies and gentlemen. You've now heard the arguments from those who oppose the suggestion made in the referendum. For the sake of objectivity, we decided it's only fair to also invite someone from the Yes campaign to state their case." The man on stage nodded at Lorcan, who appeared to stiffen more, if such a thing were possible, before getting up and slowly approaching the speaking platform. Eric's heartbeat increased as he worried about the man he loved, and he said a silent prayer to the God he didn't believe in, for the words to flow and the audience not to be too hostile. He held his breath as he waited for Lorcan to start.

"Thank you for allowing me to say a few words."

Eric released the air he'd been holding as he stared at his boyfriend—if that was still true—and recognized the nervous tension on his face. Lorcan moved his head as if he wanted to memorize the faces of everybody in the hall for future reference and yet, Eric was sure he didn't see anybody.

"I realize this isn't a comfortable subject for most of you. Trust me, it isn't easy for me, either. It never was." Lorcan paused, as if he wasn't sure how to go on, and for a moment Eric was convinced he was about to step away from the microphone and sit down again. Eric imagined he could hear Lorcan's deep sigh before he continued. "You're being asked to vote in favor of something you've always been told is wrong. Most of you are certain people like me are an abomination in the eyes of God."

Eric saw several people nod in agreement.

"But don't you feel that thinking along those lines amounts to accusing God of making countless mistakes? God, we've been told, is almighty. God is infallible. If that is true, then why are gay children being born every day? Because believe me when I say that none of us woke up one morning and decided to be gay out of spite, or out of some deep-rooted desire to be different. Far from it. When I first realized I was attracted to men, I hated myself. I didn't want to be the odd one out. All I desired was to be the same as everybody else — to fit in. And I don't. I can't begin to explain how much it hurts when you're being treated as different, less than others, just because you were born a certain way."

Lorcan paused again and Eric braced himself, convinced someone in the audience would start heckling any moment, but silence reigned supreme. Eric didn't think it would have been his approach, but maybe honest and vulnerable was the way to win over the crowd.

"We're not asking for special treatment. All we want is to be treated the same way as you. This vote isn't about whether or not you understand or approve of homosexuality. It has nothing to do with raising and adopting children. All a Yes vote would ensure is that we will be a little bit less separate from the rest of society. We just want to be equal. Nothing is going to change for you. Your marriages will still be as good or as bad as they are right now — your weddings still as lavish or as simple as you want them to be. Voting Yes won't cost you anything and will give so very much."

Lorcan looked up and his gaze sought Eric's before he bowed his head and took a small step backward.

"But what about the children!" an angry voice shouted from somewhere in the back of the hall.

Eric turned to see who had spoken but was too late. When he focused on Lorcan again the man had gone through a transformation. The hesitation was gone, and no sign of shyness or awkwardness remained as Lorcan all but glared at the crowd.

"Yes! The children. Let's talk about them. Like I said, this referendum isn't about whether or not a gay couple should be able to adopt a child. Children are already being raised by same-sex couples and legislation to facilitate that is separate from the marriage issue. But, if you are so worried about the children and their feelings, how can you possibly stand by while people proclaim, day after day, that the only way a child should be raised is by a heterosexual couple? How do you imagine that makes children who are now growing up with gay parents, or are being brought up by single parents, feel? Do you seriously believe it's a good idea to tell all those children they're just not good enough? Because that's what you're doing. Just as you're telling every child who is questioning their sexuality right now, and trying to come to terms with the fact that they don't fit what society has decided is the norm, that they're inferior. Don't tell me you're worried about the children if you're prepared to hurt so many of them just to win your argument. Don't be a hypocrite. This has nothing to do with the children and everything to do with your prejudices."

Hesitant clapping started on Eric's right and within moments others joined in. Eric's heart swelled as he watched Lorcan fully relax for the first time in four days. He had no doubt Lorcan knew as well as he did that he wouldn't have convinced everyone. But, by the sound of it, he'd managed to make at least a few people think.

Chapter Nineteen

"Give me the keys." Eric held out his hand. "You must be exhausted."

Lorcan surrendered them without a word even though he wasn't tired at all. Elated best described how he felt right now. He'd bloody done it, and if the applause and the reactions of those who had approached him afterward were anything to go by, he'd done it well. He smiled as he thought back to the moment his granny had approached him and pulled him down into a hug. "I'm so proud of you, my boy. And don't you worry. I'll make sure those old farts in my home vote the right way."

He wouldn't have been surprised if she managed it, too. The non-confrontational gran he remembered from when he'd been growing up had turned out to be a formidable force of nature.

Lost in his thoughts, Lorcan didn't notice his surroundings as he and Eric stepped away from the town hall and turned in the direction of where they'd parked Eric's car.

"Lorcan! Wait a moment, please."

The elation Lorcan had enjoyed only a moment ago vanished as soon as he recognized Father Brendan's voice. He considered ignoring the request and just walking away, but years of having been taught to respect and obey the clergy took over and, without a conscious decision on his part, Lorcan turned around and faced the approaching priest.

"Father Brendan, what can I do for you?"

Lorcan braced himself while he waited for what he was sure would be a reprimand at best but more likely a full-scale argument.

"Nothing, son. I just wanted to congratulate you on the speech you just made."

"You –" Lorcan had no idea how to continue the sentence, because he wasn't sure he could trust his ears.

The priest smiled. "Yes, I guess that would surprise you."

"Indeed," Lorcan said, having rediscovered his tongue. "My parents have made a point of telling me how your sermons have been all about the necessity for people to vote No."

To Lorcan's surprise, his statement appeared to embarrass Father Brendan.

"Yes, well, that is the Church's official stance. And us priests are expected to toe the line and share it loud and clear."

"And my words made you reconsider?" Lorcan almost snorted. "I can't imagine you're agreeing with me."

"Officially I can't, of course, son. But I tend to think you're right. If we insist that God's infallible, we also have to accept that people are born exactly the way they were meant to be."

A lifetime of Catholic indoctrination battled with Lorcan's need to know more. Taking a deep breath, he asked the question that was burning on his lips. "Does that mean you'll be telling people to vote Yes from now on?" He had no illusions about what the answer would be. The hierarchy in the Church was well established and strictly adhered to, after all. Still, he couldn't deny he was curious about the priest's answer.

"No, I'm afraid I can't do that." The regret in Father Brendan's voice sounded sincere. "But I *can* stop demanding that they vote No. It may be too little too late, but I hope it will be better than nothing."

Knock me over with a feather.

"Thank you, Father." For the first time in as long as he could remember, Lorcan actually meant the words. "I've, ah..." Lorcan glanced over to where Eric stood patiently waiting for him a few meters away.

"You've got to get home, and so do I." The priest winked. "I've got a sermon to rewrite." He held out his hand and Lorcan shook it. "Good luck, son. I'll say a prayer for you and your cause."

As he watched Father Brendan walk away, Lorcan still couldn't believe what had just happened. Of course, he'd be even more excited if he could make himself believe that his parents might go through a similar Road to Damascus experience and change their minds, but Lorcan knew that might be hoping for a miracle too many. Still, all things considered, the past ten hours hadn't been anywhere near as torturous as he'd feared and he couldn't stop himself from grinning as a result of the elation and relief he was experiencing.

He turned and approached Eric. With his mind still trying to catch up with what had just happened, he barely noticed the lack of reaction from Eric as they made their way to the carpark.

He got in the car and buckled up before turning his head and opening his mouth to share his euphoria with Eric, only to snap his lips together again when he saw the pinched look on his boyfriend's face.

Fuck.

In the aftermath of his speech, he'd completely forgotten about the mess he'd created yesterday. He stared at his hands while he tried to figure out how to fix the situation. He'd been beastly to Eric. He'd cut him off without any explanation and he'd obviously hurt him. He'd been so sure that not burdening his boyfriend with all his doubts and fears was the sensible thing to do.

Except clearly things are far from right. Maybe I'm supposed to talk about shit like this, share my feelings. Who knew? I have to say something now, but what? Where do I start? How do I approach the subject? What words should I – ?

"Would you tell me what was going on in your mind these past few days? Were you second guessing your decision, or…?"

Eric sounded hesitant and Lorcan hated himself for having put that doubt in the normally so confident man.

"No, I never considered pulling out again. It was just hard."

"What was hard?"

Lorcan reflected for a moment before answering. "You know how you and the others are always making fun of my need to be thoroughly prepared for everything I do — especially when it's something new?"

"Yes."

"Well, I couldn't prepare for this. Not really. I wasn't entirely sure whether or not I would be expected to say something until we were well into that meeting. And even if I had known for sure that I would be making a speech, I had no idea what I would be saying because I couldn't predict what I would have to react to." He paused and collected his thoughts. "Add to that the distinct possibility of running into people I didn't want to see and — Shit, I don't know. It was as if my mind shut down. My thoughts ran in circles without ever coming up with a possible answer. And the closer I got to the actual moment, the more tense I became."

"Fair enough." Eric looked at Lorcan for a moment before focusing on the road again. "But you could have talked to me."

Ouch.

The hurt Eric unsuccessfully tried to hide from his voice filled Lorcan with guilt. He should have opened up to Eric. Especially when he'd told him he preferred to be on his own last night.

"I know," Lorcan said, realizing his mistake as soon as he said the words. "I mean, obviously, I didn't know, but I should have known. Shit. I'm rambling." He leaned against the headrest for a moment and closed his eyes, trying to figure out how to continue.

"The thing is, I've always sorted issues out for myself. I never shared problems or worries with others. I've always

159

been sure my parents didn't want to hear about the feelings and thoughts that worried me when I was growing up. I told you I've never been in a relationship." Lorcan stared straight ahead, concentrating on the red lights glowing on the bumper of the car in front of them. "I never expected to be in a relationship, either."

Out of the corner of his eye, he saw Eric taking a deep breath, as if he was about to interrupt Lorcan, and he hurried on. "Not out of some inferiority complex or something like that. I was happy on my own. I liked living my life my own way, and it never felt as if I might be missing out. So" — he swallowed — "when I became all tense and frustrated about the situation I'd allowed myself to end up in, I did what I've always done. I shut myself off from the rest of the world and tried to figure it out. I've been doing it like that since I was fourteen and realized, for the first time, that I wasn't like most of the boys in my school."

"You never talked to anyone about anything?" Eric sounded stunned.

Lorcan grimaced. "Not quite that bad. I mean, if I happened to be around Troy when I found myself facing a dilemma and he asked me about it, I would talk it through. But I can't remember ever bringing an issue up with him myself. It's second nature now. I have a problem, I solve it."

Lorcan waited. He desperately wanted to ask Eric what was going on in his mind, but after everything he'd just said, he didn't have the right. If he could cut Eric off for three days without even giving it a second thought, the least he could do was allow Eric the opportunity to work his way through Lorcan's words for himself. There was something else he needed to say, though.

"I'm sorry. I hurt you. I allowed myself to fall back into old habits and never even considered what it might look or feel like for you. I'm a selfish bastard. Or maybe I was right all along. Perhaps I'm just not cut out for relationships."

He closed his eyes again as he reflected on how much of a fool he'd been. Five months ago, he'd been lecturing Troy about the importance of communication when his friend and Xander had run into trouble, and here he was behaving even worse. At least Troy had had good reasons for shutting Xander down, even if he'd read the situation wrong. Lorcan had no such excuse. Not talking to Eric, not explaining why he needed to be alone had been bad enough. The fact that he hadn't even realized how painful and confusing that had to be for Eric made it so much worse—Lorcan had no idea what to say, or how to fix it.

The prolonged silence ate at Lorcan. Clearly Eric agreed that he wasn't relationship material. And he'd be right, except that Lorcan couldn't imagine going on without Eric, nor how he would deal with having him live across the hall. So close and yet so far away.

"I just want to say one more thing, if I may." Lorcan opened his eyes in time to see Eric nod. "I want you to know that even though I didn't speak to you and sent you away last night, I could only go through with this because you were there. The only thing stopping me from walking away from that microphone tonight was your presence on that front row."

He heard the sigh as it escaped Eric and wished he knew how to interpret it. He couldn't make himself turn to Eric again. The silence surrounding them ate away at Lorcan, but after he had refused to have any background noise in the car on their way to Mullingar, it didn't seem fair to turn something on now. His leg jerked when Eric squeezed it softly.

"Jaysus, Lorcan." Eric sounded weary. "The past few days have been"—he paused for a moment—"far from easy."

Lorcan recognized an understatement when he heard it. "Don't you mean hard, cruel, tortuous, fucked-up even?"

Eric's soft chuckle relieved some of the tension knotting Lorcan's stomach. "Yeah. That, too." He sighed. "It's not that I have a problem with you wanting to figure things out for yourself, not really. But when you shut me out last night, when you wouldn't even look at me, shit, I don't know, I figured I'd missed something."

"Missed something?" Lorcan asked the question, well aware that he probably didn't want to hear the answer.

Eric glanced his way before responding. "Don't play stupid. You're well aware what I mean. Ever since I came back we've spent every free minute together. What was I supposed to think when you suddenly turned around and told me you didn't want to be near me?"

"You thought I wanted to end our relationship?" Lorcan had trouble breathing. The idea that Eric might interpret his actions like that had never occurred to him. "God, no. I mean, quite the opposite in fact. I needed to be alone because it didn't seem fair to burden you with my problems — problems I'd created myself, at that. And you see me too clearly."

"What the fuck does that mean?"

Eric's choice of words underlined how incredibly wrong and potentially damaging Lorcan's decisions had been, and he swallowed hard while considering how to answer. "I can't get away with anything when you are around. You look at me and you see through me. With you I can't pretend that I'm fine when I'm not. If you'd stayed with me last night I would have ended up spilling everything I had on my mind, and I wanted to avoid that."

"Because you didn't want to burden me. How noble of you." The cynicism in Eric's voice stabbed at Lorcan's heart. "I don't suppose it occurred to you that having me worry about whether or not I still had a boyfriend would be a far greater burden."

Lorcan groaned as he closed his eyes again. Why had he not realized Eric might interpret his lack of communication and need to be alone as a sign of a dying relationship? "I'm an eejit."

"You certainly acted like one." Eric's words would have been worrying if it hadn't been for the trace of humor in his voice.

"I'm sorry." Lorcan forced himself to keep his gaze fixed

on Eric as he spoke. "It shouldn't surprise me that you interpreted my actions like that. I may be inexperienced at relationships, but I'm not stupid." He swallowed in an effort to dislodge the shame choking him. "I guess I was so caught up in my personal drama, I never gave any thought to how it would come across to you."

Eric stayed silent as he steered the car onto their street and into a parking bay.

"Let's finish this conversation upstairs."

Lorcan nodded, got out of the car and followed Eric through the front door, up the stairs and straight into Eric's apartment. He waited quietly as Eric walked to the fridge and extracted two cans of lager, before handing one to Lorcan. His mind was awash with thoughts, partial sentences, apologies and excuses as Eric crossed the room and lowered himself to the couch.

"Are you just going to stand there?" Eric patted the couch in invitation.

Lorcan sat, and stared at the can in his hands. He had so many words in his head and no idea which ones to use.

"Let's get one thing clear." Eric's voice was calm and businesslike, sending fearful shivers down Lorcan's spine. "You are not breaking up with me, right?"

"Right." Lorcan directed his words at the drink in his hands. "Unless you...I mean, I wouldn't blame you if..." He trailed off, sure Eric would have gotten his meaning and unable to make himself finish either of those sentences.

"Lorcan, it would help if you looked at me."

Lorcan lifted his chin and turned to the side to find Eric studying him.

"You're right. I do find it easy to read your emotions and thoughts from your face. Right now, I sorta need that."

"Okay." It took all Lorcan had not to study his hands again, but honoring Eric's request was the least he could do. The hesitant smile on Eric's face made it a little bit easier to hold his gaze.

"Let me answer your unasked question for you. No, I

do not want to stop being with you. Everybody is entitled to make a mistake. But I don't want to go through what happened last night ever again, either." Eric's tone of voice made it perfectly clear he was deadly serious. "If you have an issue, you tell me. If you want to spend a night on your own, that's fine..." Eric laughed. "Actually, it's not. I missed having you in my bed. But if that's what you need, I can live with it. Provided I'm sure it's only about wanting to be on your own and not something worse. Don't leave me guessing and coming up with all sorts of worst-case scenarios. I'm too old to play teenage games."

Shame flooded Lorcan. Eric was right. He had been behaving like a stupid kid.

"Come here." Eric pointed at his lap.

Lorcan studied Eric's face, unsure he'd understood the request correctly. Then he was up like a shot. Desperate to close the distance he'd created between them, Lorcan lowered himself until he sat on Eric's thighs, his lover's handsome face only a short distance from his.

"I'm so sorry," he whispered the words, before tentatively bringing his face closer to Eric's, who sat still and waited. Relief flooded through Lorcan when he pressed his mouth against Eric's and had his kiss returned. He parted his lips and brushed the tip of his tongue over Eric's until they separated and Lorcan could push his tongue into Eric's mouth. It was the first kiss they'd ever shared all over again. Giddy pleasure, surprise it was actually happening and pure delight that he'd been lucky enough to have this man in his life threatened to overwhelm him. He wrapped his hand around the back of Eric's neck and deepened the kiss while he stroked soft skin with his fingertips until Eric sighed.

"May I ask you something?" Lorcan interrupted the kiss but pressed his forehead to Eric's, unwilling to completely sever the physical contact between them.

"Sure." Eric's face relaxed into a lazy smile.

"Why did you still come with me today? I mean, after

what I put you through and what you thought it meant, why didn't you just pull out and leave me to sort it out on my own?"

"You really don't get it, do you?" Eric asked.

"Get what?"

"Relationships," Eric replied. "When I'm serious about a relationship I don't just walk away. I don't give up on the spur of the moment." He smirked. "If you want to get rid of me, it's going to take more than being short with me and making me sleep on my own."

Lorcan stared at the amazing man in front of him, lost for words.

"But, Lorcan, I would have gone with you even if I had been sure you were breaking up with me. This is important to you. I was never going to let you face this alone."

Lorcan opened his mouth to interrupt, but Eric beat him to it.

"I know. Its importance is far wider than just you, but that's not my focus right now. You are. I'd told you I would go with you, so I went." He shrugged. "Besides, I wanted to have this conversation and realized there would be no point starting it before you had what you thought would be an ordeal behind you. So I came. And I'm glad I did. You were magnificent."

Lorcan didn't mind at all that his face betrayed his feelings once again when a huge grin spread across it. "Magnificent, huh?" He gazed into Eric's eyes and drowned in the depth of feeling he encountered. He stroked his thumb across Eric's lips before once more kissing him, long and deep.

"I love you." He hadn't said it often enough. From now on, he'd make it his mission to let Eric know exactly how important he was. He never wanted there to be any doubt again. "I've been in love with you almost since the moment we met. I loved you last night when I refused to talk to you and sent you away. I fooled myself into believing it was the loving thing to do." He pressed his finger against Eric's lips again to stop him from speaking. "I won't make that mistake again. I love you and I don't want to risk losing this…you. Ever."

Lorcan held his breath as he stared at Eric, who gazed back at him in wonder.

"You've got a strange way of showing it," Eric murmured, then took the sting out of his words by claiming Lorcan's lips and demanding entry with his tongue.

Lorcan imagined he could taste the last tendrils of anger and frustration in Eric's kiss before it softened into something more intimate and sexy. He shuffled closer to Eric until his crotch pressed into his lover's, and ground against him shamelessly.

Eric was breathless when he pulled back from the kiss. "One more thing."

Lorcan steeled himself to receive whatever might be said with good grace.

"I love you, too, you big eejit."

As their mouths reconnected, Lorcan felt as if he was flying. Emotional rollercoaster didn't begin to describe the twenty-four hours he'd just had, but to get to this ending he'd live them all over again with a smile on his face. When they came up for air there was only one thing on his mind.

"Take me to bed?"

Eric pushed Lorcan off his lap and got up, a broad grin shining on his face. "With pleasure. And you'll be lucky if I let you go again."

I'll be lucky if you don't. Lorcan grabbed Eric's hand and all but ran the few steps to the bedroom he'd denied himself the previous night.

Chapter Twenty

Eric knew something — or rather somebody — was missing as soon as he woke up. He felt around with his hand, without opening his eyes, thinking maybe Lorcan had moved to the edge of the bed, but soon realized he was indeed on his own. It was a strange experience. He and Lorcan had spent the grand total of three nights apart since his return. They'd fallen asleep together last night as well, Eric the big spoon to Lorcan's little one.

He wondered where Lorcan was. Usually Eric was awake and up much earlier than his boyfriend, who seemed to have a special talent for sleep-ins and lie-ons. He opened his eyes and squinted against the light, which was much brighter than he'd expected it to be. Turning over, he found the solution to both the mystery of the missing boyfriend and the question about the unusual brightness. Lorcan had opened the curtains and stood in front of the window with his phone in his hand.

"What's with all the early morning activity?"

Lorcan turned around with a huge smile on his face. "Morning. See that?" He pointed at the grayish sky outside. "It's dry. And according to the weather forecast it won't rain at all today."

Eric's sluggish mind took a moment to catch up. Then it hit him — referendum day. "That's great news." He smiled, because it was all but impossible not to get caught up in Lorcan's obvious delight. "Whatever happens next, the weather won't be what spoils the party. But…" He allowed the sentence to trail off, curious to see if Lorcan would catch on.

"But what?"

"Are you sure you want to show yourself in all your pride and glory to every passerby this morning?"

"Oh." Lorcan bowed his head and studied his glorious naked body as if he'd been unaware of the fact he was starkers. When he looked up again he had a mischievous glint in his eyes. "Oh, well, if anybody saw, I hope they enjoyed the view."

"I sure do," Eric said. "Come back here. We're in no hurry and I want my early morning cuddle."

Lorcan grinned and walked back to the bed, his cock filling with every step he took, while Eric reflected on the advantages of an extra day off work. They'd both taken a day's annual leave. For Lorcan it had been a case of knowing he wouldn't be able to concentrate if he went in. Eric, on the other hand, hadn't been able to pass up the opportunity to spend an extra full day with Lorcan.

Lorcan pulled back the covers and all but threw himself onto the mattress next to Eric, pushing as close as he possibly could.

"Fuck, man, you're freezing." Eric shivered.

"Yeah, well. I said it was dry." Lorcan grinned. "Not that it's warm. Although, that should be okay as well later on."

"Good, we'll get up later then." Eric maneuvered the slowly warming Lorcan until he was lying on top of him. Lorcan gazed into Eric's eyes. "I'm glad it will be over after today. Well, tomorrow," he corrected himself. "Waiting for the result is going to be a bitch, but at least there's nothing we can do anymore. It will either pass or it won't."

Eric stroked a hand through Lorcan's messy, sleep-tousled hair. He had no doubt that Lorcan would be devastated if the result would turn out to be negative, but his lover was right. Whatever happened next, it was out of their hands. All they could do now was go to the polling station, add their own vote to those of others and hope it would be enough.

"You know, I still can't get over all these people coming

home from all over the world just to vote in the referendum."

Eric nodded. He'd been tied to his Twitter account for the past two days as ever more people announced in one hundred and forty characters or less that they'd landed in Ireland for a flying visit, just to cast their vote. As far as he could tell, distance and money hadn't been an issue, either. People had flown in from America and Australia as well as from the European continent.

"I don't think it has ever happened before," Lorcan continued. "I mean, they never cared enough to invest in a ticket and undertake a long journey just to support or oppose a certain cause in the past. And no way are all of them gay," Lorcan all but gushed. "For the first time, I'm allowing myself to think we might actually do it."

Eric laughed. "You're crazy. The polls have been giving the result to the Yes side for months, and only now are you willing to believe it will happen?"

"Polls are just a big waste of paper. You know that as well as I do." Lorcan frowned. "How often did they get it wrong in the past? More often than they got it right, I bet. But" — his face brightened again — "all these people entering the country today wouldn't even have been taken into account for those polls. So, yes, I may be late to the party, but I am turning into a believer."

Lorcan moved into a more comfortable position on Eric's outstretched form. "Anyway, enough about that. There'll be more than enough time to worry about the results later on. Right now, I'm more in the mood for this."

Lorcan lowered his head and took Eric's earlobe between his lips. Using the tip of his tongue he traced the sensitive outline, and Eric shivered. God, his man knew exactly how to drive him crazy. Not a single erogenous zone on Eric's body had escaped Lorcan's scrutiny and he used and abused them to his best advantage.

Lorcan moved again and when their cocks rubbed against each other Eric was sure it wasn't by accident. Not that he had any objections. To prove how much he didn't mind,

Eric grabbed Lorcan's arse with both hands and pulled him closer. "God, you feel good." He groaned when Lorcan bit into his earlobe before licking the sting away again.

There was a lot to be said for sleeping naked, Eric pondered, as he explored all the skin available to him. Lorcan couldn't stay still and the constant stimulation did wonderful things to Eric's cock. If the sounds Lorcan emitted were anything to go by, he was on the same page.

"What do you want?" Lorcan whispered the question into Eric's ear.

"You inside me." Eric held his breath as he waited for Lorcan's response. Lorcan had said he was versatile, but so far he'd only bottomed, and Eric had had no issue with that at all. Right now, all he could think of was feeling Lorcan's cock deep inside him, stimulating him in ways he hadn't been for longer than he cared to remember.

Lorcan stared into Eric's eyes for a while and for a moment he thought his lover would deny him. Then a dirty grin spread across Lorcan's face. He slid down Eric's body until he was nestled, on his knees, between Eric's spread legs.

"Can you reach the drawer?" Lorcan's voice was husky and had a hungry undertone.

Eric stretched and only just managed to grab the lube and condoms. As soon as he'd dumped them on the bed, Lorcan manhandled him until he was on his hands and knees with his arse in the air.

"If I'm going to do this…" Lorcan stroked Eric's backside, not stopping until he reached his balls and fondled them. "I'm going to do it right."

Lorcan grabbed his arse cheeks and pulled them apart. Warm air ghosted across his hole and Eric would have been ashamed of the whimper escaping his lips if he hadn't been too busy losing himself in the amazing sensation. At the first lick of Lorcan's wet tongue, Eric dropped his head to the pillow and surrendered to the sensations. Over his hole, down his crack, across his taint, teasing his balls. Cold air stimulated the damp skin only just abandoned, while

Lorcan used his masterful tongue to provide wet heat to another spot. He was dimly aware of one hand leaving his arse cheek and sucked in a deep breath when it wrapped around his straining cock, a finger spreading pre-cum over the sensitive head. Between the tip of Lorcan's tongue entering him and the firm strokes his lover's fist delivered to his dick, Eric feared he'd come any second. *So good.*

"Jaysus, Lorcan. You're killing me."

Lorcan removed his mouth long enough to chuckle, the evil sound only adding to Eric's excitement. "You don't get to die yet."

He heard the sound of foil ripping followed by lube being squirted, and tensed in exited expectation.

"How long has it been?" The question was matter-of-fact, but Lorcan's voice betrayed his own excitement.

"Too long." Consumed by the mind-blowing sensuality of Lorcan's ministrations, Eric couldn't gather his thoughts, never mind do the math. He wondered why he topped most of the time, and one well-lubed finger entering his narrow passage later, he silently vowed that it wouldn't be as long until it happened again.

Lorcan took his time and Eric found himself caught between gratitude and a desperate need for more. When, after what felt like centuries, the head of Lorcan's cock pressed against his hole, he hissed. "Yes. Please, yes."

It really had been too long. The stretch bordered on painful until it wasn't anymore. Lorcan slowly pushed all the way in, enfolding Eric in his arms when he reached his destination. The movements in and out were slow, sensuous, and Eric lost himself in the almost forgotten sensations. Moans and groans filled the room and Eric had no idea which were his and which came from Lorcan's mouth. His whole universe was centered on the point where he and Lorcan connected. Surely this was as close as a man could come to Heaven without dying. He didn't think it could get any better until Lorcan once again circled his fingers around Eric's cock. His movements became faster and harder, and with every motion Eric's cock slid through Lorcan's hand, still covered in lube.

"Come for me, lover." Lorcan's breath was warm against his ear. The subsequent soft bite on Eric's shoulder sent him over the edge while he cried out and cursed as his arms gave way and his upper body dropped to the mattress.

"Fuck. Eric!" Lorcan shouted as his rhythm became erratic.

When Lorcan collapsed on top of him, Eric had recovered enough presence of mind to roll them both to the side so he didn't land in the sticky mess his orgasm had left on the sheet.

"Now that's how you start referendum day." Minutes passed in silence, only disturbed by the sound of two men trying to catch their breaths, before Eric smiled at Lorcan and kissed him softly. "I'm starving. How about a shower and breakfast?"

Lorcan returned both the smile and the kiss before nodding and pushing himself up. "Sounds like a plan." He grinned. "We'll have to do this again someday soon."

* * * *

Several hours later, as they left the polling station after having cast their votes, Eric still luxuriated in the afterglow of a morning well spent. Between the early morning sex, a joint shower, extravagant breakfast and a leisurely stroll through town, it was easy to believe they were celebrating a holiday rather than going out to do their civic duty. Of course, none of that guaranteed that they'd feel as good tomorrow. More than twenty-four hours stood between them and the announcement of the result. And if, God forbid, he was wrong and the Yes vote didn't make the day—his stomach squeezed just contemplating the idea— Eric wasn't sure how either of them would react.

"Are you okay?" Lorcan studied him with concern etched on his face.

"Sure, why?" Eric asked, although he was pretty sure he knew what had caused the question.

"You suddenly looked worried," Lorcan said. "I mean, one second you were smiling happily and the next you had this frown on your face. Don't tell me you're starting to have doubts now."

Eric stopped walking and turned to Lorcan, unable to stop himself from grinning. "And here I had myself convinced you were the only one with the easy-to-read expressions. So much for my man-of-mystery image. Clearly, you see right through me in the same way I can tell what's going on in your head."

Lorcan smiled back at him while shaking his head. "Nah, I don't think so. What you do is almost scary. I doubt there's anything I could keep hidden from you."

"You'd better not." Eric kept his tone light while making sure the message came across. "We've both seen where that leaves us. I'd rather not go through that again." He felt guilty about mentioning their one fight when Lorcan sighed and turned his head. "Sorry. I'm not going to keep on beating you over the head with that. I shouldn't have mentioned it."

"It's okay." Lorcan shrugged. "I did something stupid and you've every right to pull me up on it."

"Not anymore. I had my say, we worked it out, and that is enough. I won't mention it again. I promise," Eric swore to himself he'd keep his word. Clearly that episode had hit him harder than he'd realized, but that still didn't give him the right to use it as a weapon.

Lorcan taking his hand for a moment and squeezing it surprised Eric. His boyfriend wasn't usually prone to public displays of affection.

"Listen, if I'm going to be a dick, you earn the right to mention it." Lorcan grinned. "Just remember that if the shoe's ever on the other foot, I'll be the first to remind you of your foolishness. Now, how about a drink? Voting is thirsty work and I don't feel like going home yet."

Eric studied their surroundings and noticed that they'd stopped in front of their local pub. "Is this supposed to be a coincidence?"

"Maybe." Lorcan grinned. "We're here, so let's go for a pint."

As they moved from the bar to a table in the corner of the pub, Lorcan's phone made a message-received sound. Eric watched Lorcan's face as he read the words on the screen.

"Well, I'll be damned."

"What?"

Lorcan lifted his gaze, confusion clear in his eyes. "I don't believe this. That's from my dad, who's just informed me that he — wait for it — voted Yes after all." Lorcan picked up his pint and downed about a third of it in one swallow.

"That's great news, isn't it?" Eric didn't understand why Lorcan wasn't dancing on the table for joy. "Didn't I tell you not to give up on your parents?"

Lorcan grimaced and nodded. "Yes, it is wonderful, and, yes, you did tell me not to write them off. It would have been even better if he hadn't ended his message with the words, *please don't tell your mother.*"

Not for the first time, Eric tried to imagine what it might feel like to not have unconditional love and support from his parents, and once again he failed. His life hadn't been split in two as Lorcan's had. There had been no before and after coming out for him. Not having the support he'd taken for granted all these years had to be devastating. On the other hand...

"Don't go looking for miracles, Lorcan." Eric searched his mind for the best words to use. "A few hours ago you were still convinced he would vote against the referendum. A few months ago, you didn't think you'd ever introduce your partner to your parents, or anybody in your family for that matter." He inspected the rest of the pub and placed his hand over Lorcan's on the table. "Twice now he has surprised you. Sure, they may be small steps, but at least they're heading in the right direction. Who knows what might happen next."

As if on cue, Lorcan's phone lit up again. Eric watched Lorcan as he read the message. A surprise-filled expression flashed across his face immediately followed by his lips stretching into a broad smile. "Well, fuck me."

"Yes, please," Eric deadpanned with a wink. "What's up?"

"That one's from my mother." Lorcan grinned again before muttering, "I didn't even realize she knew how to text." He looked at Eric with delight written all over his handsome features. "It's not as spectacular as my father's message, but still…"

"Well, don't keep me in suspense," Eric said. "What's the message?"

"She's decided not to vote at all. She says that while she still doesn't feel marriage equality is right, she couldn't make herself vote in a way that might hurt one of her children." Lorcan stared at his phone as if it held the answers to all the mysteries in the universe.

"I never told you, did I?" Eric asked.

"Tell me what?"

"That I saw your parents in that hall in Mullingar." Eric recognized the surprise on Lorcan's face and continued. "I saw them while we were waiting for the meeting to get started but didn't want to say anything in case it would make you more nervous than you already were."

"Good call," Lorcan muttered.

"I had every intention of telling you afterward, but then with that whole mess we needed to clear up…"

"My mess, you mean," Lorcan said, a shadow passing over his face.

"Your mess. My mess. Who cares?" Eric shrugged. "It's behind us now. We've talked about it, dealt with it, so there's no point in continuing to feel bad about it. But they were there."

"I bet you that was my gran's doing."

"That wouldn't surprise me at all." Eric laughed. "Still,

she wasn't with them in that voting booth. To vote in favor or not vote at all was their decision alone." He paused, his features turning serious again. "Like I said, small steps. Given that they're heading in the right direction, I think we've got a good reason to celebrate. Want another one?" He nodded at the now empty pint glasses.

"Yes, please, but I'll get these."

While Lorcan approached the bar to get their order in, Eric reflected that a weight seemed to have lifted off his lover's shoulders. A national victory might still be up in the air, but personal triumphs had been achieved and, regardless of what would happen tomorrow, nobody could take that away from Lorcan.

Chapter Twenty-One

"If they allow any more people in, we'll be squashed."

Lorcan glanced at Xander before studying his surroundings again. The courtyard of Dublin Castle was bursting at the seams. It was hard to judge, but if he had to guess, Lorcan would have said there were at least two-thousand other people there besides him and his friends.

"If I'm going to drown in a sea of people I'd just as soon it happens on a happy occasion," Eric said.

Lorcan leaned into his boyfriend and smiled up at him. "Don't go counting our chickens just yet. I'll grant you all the signs are positive, but it's not official yet."

"Tell that to the other people here," Eric replied.

He has a point. Lorcan couldn't deny that the atmosphere surrounding them could be best described as festive, jubilant even. The square was awash with rainbow flags, silver balloons forming the word *yes*, and people holding colored cards with the word *Equal* on them. The very air he breathed appeared to be infused with happiness.

"Explain this to me again. Both your parents texted you separately?"

Troy's question pulled Lorcan out of his happy musing and he turned to face his friend, fully expecting to see relief and delight on his face, too, and surprised not to find it.

"And your mother decided not to vote at all while your father voted Yes but doesn't want you to tell your mother?" Troy shook his head, a half-smile tugging at his lips. "I'm delighted for you, mate, but, Jaysus, your parents are behaving like little kids."

Lorcan studied his friend, wondering if there might

be more going on than Troy taking advantage of an opportunity to slag him off. "You know what they're like, Troy. I'm taking this as a step in the right direction. Sure, I could overthink it and come to the conclusion that it's too little too late, but why would I?"

Troy shrugged and looked away, the smile gone from his face, and suddenly Lorcan got it.

"Have you any idea how your da voted?"

Troy turned back and faced Lorcan with a frown on his face. "I'm not even sure he went out to vote, never mind how."

Lorcan searched for words to make his friend feel better as Xander dropped his hand on Troy's shoulder and squeezed his partner softly. Troy leaned into Xander and visibly relaxed.

"I watched those videos of people going to their parents and talking about the referendum, and I considered it." Troy shrugged. "I decided to leave well enough alone, though. I mean, I never imagined he'd meet or accept a man I might hook up with, and he welcomed Xander into his house. Even if he did vote against equality, that acceptance is something to build on. I don't want to create a new barrier between us by asking questions he may not want to answer."

"Fair enough," Lorcan said. "I didn't want to go all heavy on you. I guess I figured it was a foregone conclusion after he'd accepted Xander, but I totally get why you didn't ask. I didn't even consider asking mine again, despite Father Brendan saying he wouldn't be advocating for a No vote any longer. They'd already told me they couldn't support the referendum because it was against their faith and I didn't expect them to change their mind so late in the day. To say those messages yesterday took me by surprise would be a gross understatement."

"Why is this taking so long? Is this normal?" Chris asked, frustration clear in his voice. "We've been here for hours. How hard can it be to separate the yeses from the noes?

"Yeah." Eric grimaced. "Unfortunately, we're very good at dragging out the counting process. It's frustrating. But at least the individual results from the various districts have all been positive so far."

Xander listened as Eric explained the Irish voting system to their Australian friend while he reflected the wait would have been even more frustrating if everything didn't point at a positive outcome. Within twenty minutes after the counting of the votes had started at nine in the morning, the early tallies had indicated a comfortable win for the Yes vote. When the most vocal No group had conceded defeat before midday, a huge wave of relief had passed through Lorcan. He wouldn't completely relax until the official, nationwide result had been announced, but his hope had flared up into something bordering on certainty and he had a hard time containing his excitement.

"Hmmm," Chris grumbled when Eric finished his explanation, "still think it could be done more efficiently. Then again, no matter how long it takes, at least you got to vote on the subject. In Australia, they're showing no signs of introducing marriage equality."

"What?"

Despite the crowds around them making movement difficult, Xander, Troy, Eric and Lorcan turned to face Chris.

"I thought... I assumed..." Lorcan stared at Chris while he tried to process what the man had just said. "If anybody had asked me, I would have said Australia had had it in place for years. Wow." Pride swelled in Lorcan's chest as he realized how truly special it would be if — no, when — the announcement would be made. Who would have thought Roman Catholic Ireland would be at the forefront of the equality movement?

Eric placed his arm around Lorcan's shoulder and pulled him closer. For a moment Lorcan stiffened, relaxing again as soon as he realized this was probably the safest location and occasion for public displays of affection he'd ever find himself in.

"It can't be much longer now," Eric said the words softly, his lips brushing Lorcan's cheek as he spoke, sending a shiver down his spine. "Are you a believer yet?"

Lorcan turned his head and smiled at Eric. "I am. I have been for a few hours. I still can't wait for the official announcement, though." He lightly kissed Eric's cheek before focusing on the balustrade at the top of the courtyard again.

A host of politicians, celebrities and, most importantly of all, Panti Bliss, the unofficial spokesperson and figurehead of the Yes campaign, had already made their appearance there. Nobody was in any doubt what the outcome would be, and everybody was patiently waiting to have it confirmed as six o'clock came and went.

"Hey, look over there." The surprise in Chris's voice made Lorcan turn around to discover what he was talking about. "Didn't we do tattoos for those lads recently?"

"That's right," Troy said after studying the couple a short distance away from them. "Remember, Xander? You worked on the design one of them brought in."

Lorcan stared at the young couple and realized they were the same two lads who'd been in Troy's tattoo shop the afternoon he and Eric had gotten their tattoos. They'd been cute then and they were even cuter today, with their rainbow-colored T-shirts, holding hands and grinning from ear to ear. He turned to point them out to Eric when a hush fell over the crowd.

A gray-haired woman appeared on the big plasma screen in front of Dublin Castle — the moment of truth had arrived and despite all his doubts having disappeared over the past few hours, Lorcan suddenly felt slightly sick. *What if…?*

Just a few short minutes later the courtyard had transformed into a jubilant, dancing, crying, laughing sea of bodies. More than sixty-percent of the population had voted in favor. Lorcan swayed on his feet as he tried to process the news. Only one polling station had closed with a majority against.

"Hey, I told you we'd win." Eric brushed the tears from Lorcan's cheek before pulling him into a tight hug.

"You did, and I should have listened to you!" Lorcan took Eric's face in his hands and pressed their mouths together. He couldn't imagine ever being entirely comfortable indulging in public displays of affection but today it felt right. The kiss didn't last nearly long enough for Lorcan's liking. The crowd around them moved too much, pushing him and Eric closer together and almost separating them again as people jumped, danced and embraced one another. Reluctantly, Lorcan released Eric's face and pulled back a little.

"We'll celebrate later." Eric winked. "In private."

"I'm gonna go to Capel Street," Chris announced. "From what I hear, everybody is going to PantiBar for a celebration. You lot coming along?"

While Troy and Xander enthusiastically agreed to the plan, Lorcan looked at Eric, who slowly shook his head.

"No, we'll walk with you, but I think we'll go on home," Lorcan said. "Don't get me wrong, I'm delighted with the result and I agree it deserves a good party, but it will have to happen without me. I'm drained." The moment he said the words, Lorcan knew they were true. Months of campaigning, worrying and being upset with his parents had taken their toll. Now that the fight was over, he needed some time to calm down again. A street party in the middle of Dublin would not be the right time or place for him to rediscover his equilibrium.

They slowly made their way through the celebrating crowd toward the exit of Dublin Castle's courtyard, frequently forced to stop when complete strangers pulled one or more of them in for hugs.

"This," Xander said, "is the closest I've ever come to being trapped on an emotional rollercoaster."

Lorcan knew exactly what Xander meant. Bright smiles stood side by side with tear-streaked cheeks. Expressions of heartfelt relief competed with triumphant glares. Some people pumped the air with their fists while others stood silently, drinking it all in with a faint smile tugging at their lips. In fact, the people surrounding him were a visible expression of all the conflicting emotions assaulting Lorcan. He felt connected to every single one of the men and women surrounding them, and yet he experienced the result as a personal victory, too.

"No time like the present," Chris said while pointing to the right, where a woman with rainbow-colored hair went down on one knee in front of a slightly younger-looking lady, who appeared to be unable to stop herself from nodding, her hand covering her mouth as happy tears flowed.

Leaving the courtyard took longer than it would have on any other day, but he didn't mind. Lorcan wanted to imprint these scenes on his memories. A fierce sense of being part of history, of having helped to create this moment, filled him with pride and gratitude. While he knew that today's result would not mean that the world would be perfect from now on, he allowed himself to believe, for the first time in his life, that he was indeed the equal of every other citizen of Ireland.

Five minutes of slowly shuffling their way down Parliament Street later, they passed The Front Lounge bar, where a party had started both inside and on the sidewalk. In fact, as they moved on, it became clear the whole inner city, regardless of gender or orientation, was celebrating. Cars driving by beeped their horns and people cheered and waved at one another. Anybody not knowing any better would be forgiven for thinking they'd wandered into an early celebration of Dublin Pride.

"It's just as well we want to go to PantiBar," Troy muttered as the stream of people all heading in the same direction dictated both where they were going and how fast they would get there. They allowed the festive crowd to steer them along, guide them over the river Liffey and down Capel Street, where loud voices and even louder music indicated they were heading toward the street party to end all street parties.

When they reached their destination Lorcan breathed a sigh of relief that he'd already announced he wouldn't be staying. No matter how much the colorful crowd of celebrating people mirrored his delight, he couldn't imagine immersing himself in their midst.

"Are you sure you won't stay for a drink or two?" Xander turned from Eric to Lorcan as he asked the question.

Lorcan tilted his head and studied Eric's face. As much as he didn't fancy entering the melee, he wouldn't press his point if Eric felt differently. Relief flooded through him when Eric smiled and shook his head.

"No, you're okay. I'm all peopled out," Eric said. "I'm taking my man home for a more private celebration."

"Some people have no stamina," Troy smirked, but the look in his eyes was understanding as he pulled Lorcan into a hug. "I'll call you tomorrow and tell you exactly what you missed."

"You do that," Lorcan laughed. "See you later."

"We may never do this again," Eric said a few minutes later, when they'd left most of the crowd and noise behind them, "but today I'm holding your hand all the way home."

Lorcan squeezed the fingers entwined with his, suddenly aware that they'd walked all the way from Dublin Castle like that, without giving it a second thought. As they waited for an opportunity to cross the street, a car drove by slowly, its windows wide open. A grinning man stared at them before he shouted, "When's the date, lads?"

Lorcan smiled and glanced at Eric. "That's right. Maybe I will call you my husband instead of my boyfriend one day."

Stunned silence followed his announcement before Eric laughed. "Did you just propose to me?"

"Not really." Lorcan grinned. "Don't worry about it. When I do propose, you won't need to ask. It will be more than obvious." He bit his lip as he wondered whether or not now would be the right time to mention the idea he'd been playing with for a few days.

"What's up?" Eric asked. "I recognize that face. You're worried about something, and this time it's not the referendum."

Lorcan wasn't sure whether to be grateful or frustrated that Eric once again read him so easily. He had no idea what he would do if he ever had something he really needed to keep secret from the man.

"I've been thinking," Lorcan said after they'd walked in silence for a few minutes.

"About marriage?"

"No, not marriage exactly." Lorcan's tried to keep his expression smooth but could feel his mouth twitching as it always did when he tried to keep himself from laughing nervously.

"Well, spit it out," Eric suggested.

"I figured... I mean I thought maybe..." Lorcan looked at the pavement rather than Eric in the hope that would make it easier for him to say what was on his mind. "This is probably very presumptuous of me, but with you losing your office space and the two of us basically living together in two apartments, I figured we could turn one of them into office space for you and live in the other? As in, together."

When Eric didn't make a sound, Lorcan came to a standstill, forcing Eric to do the same, before studying his boyfriend's face. Eric just stared at Lorcan, mouth slightly opened and his eyes widened.

"I mean, I'm not expecting you to agree with me or jump on the suggestion." Words fell out of Lorcan's mouth so fast he almost stumbled over them. "It's probably too soon for a move like that, if you ever want to make it, that is. And I realize there are practical considerations because you don't own your apartment yet but..."

"Hold on." Eric placed a finger over Lorcan's lips, effectively stopping his flow of words. "I happen to love your idea. I have absolutely no objection to the two of us officially moving in together, regardless of what we do with the other apartment."

He paused to study Lorcan's face as if he was looking for answers there. "Are you sure it's what you want? Wouldn't it be too much, too soon for you?"

Lorcan bent toward Eric and kissed him softly, momentarily forgetting they were on a public street, and no longer surrounded by other gay people and their supporters. "Yes, I'm sure." He repeated the kiss before continuing. "I'm also sure there's bound to be hiccups. I mean, this whole relationship thing is new for me." He hesitated, reluctant to bring it up again while at the same time wanting to make it perfectly clear that he would understand it if Eric didn't share his enthusiasm. "As if that's something I need to remind you of. But I believe it would work. I mean, maybe I needed that Mullingar episode and me fucking everything up to show me exactly what it means to be in a relationship. I'm not saying I'll never fuck up again. But I think…hope that when I do, I'll deal with it better." Out of breath and words, Lorcan stopped talking, wondering whether he'd said too much or not enough.

A smile slowly spread across Eric's face. "I have no doubt both of us will fuck up from time to time. We wouldn't be human if we didn't. And as much as I hated what happened before and after Mullingar, it did tell us one thing."

Lorcan stared at Eric dumbfounded.

"It showed us that we are able to fix things after we've fucked up." Eric pressed his lips against Lorcan's before turning and walking on. "Now let's get home. You've just given us another reason to have a long, private celebration."

Renewal

Excerpt

Chapter One

Shane accepted his change from the barman, picked up his pint and turned around. The pub was all but deserted and he had his choice of empty tables. Hardly surprising, given that it was eight o'clock on a Wednesday evening, but that didn't lessen the small stab of disappointment he felt. The first opportunity he'd had to go out in three weeks, probably the last in the foreseeable future, and not a familiar face in sight.

Not that he necessarily wanted to run into anybody who knew him well. He'd rather not answer questions about why he was never around these days. On the other hand, he desperately needed a distraction, something to take his mind off the situation he found himself in. A vaguely familiar face, somebody he could join and pass an hour or two with without running the risk of the conversation turning heavy or personal would have been perfect — and clearly wasn't happening tonight. A hook-up was even less likely and he could do with one. It had been months since he'd gotten off through means other than his own hand.

He pushed the thought to the back of his mind as he glanced around again, trying to figure out where to take his drink. The idea of sitting at one of the round tables on his own filled him with a heaviness he didn't want to explore. Shane pulled a barstool toward himself with his foot and sat. Staring into the mirror behind the bar, he took a long drink from his glass as he remembered the scene he'd left behind at home.

'Where you're going, Uncle Shane?' Five-year-old Danny had sounded close to tears even before Shane answered.

'Out for a drink, boy.' Shane had stroked the still-wet blond hair.

'Are you coming back?' The big tears welling in Danny's eyes had almost made him reconsider his idea. He couldn't blame the child for no longer trusting the adults in his life to come back after they left. He'd knelt and made sure to make eye contact before answering.

'Of course I'll come back. We're in this together, right?' He'd forced a smile in the hope it would quell the lad's growing panic. 'When you wake up tomorrow morning I'll be making you breakfast. Just as I did today. I promise. Besides, don't you like it when your granny minds you? Doesn't she let you stay up late?'

The combination of a triumphant smile and tears on the five year old's face had almost broken Shane's resolve. Christ, but I love the nipper.

'On you go, son.' His mother's voice had put an end to the conversation with Danny. 'Don't you worry about anything at all. Go and enjoy yourself for a while.'

'Sure, Ma, thanks. Don't keep him up too late.' He'd given Danny a hug and a kiss before getting up and walking out of the door, grateful for his mother's support. The situation was even harder on her than it was for Shane and not for the first time he wondered how long she'd be able to keep

up the pace.

Irritated with himself, Shane picked up his pint again and drank some more. Spending his evening worrying about the situation at home defeated the purpose of the exercise. He was supposed to get a short reprieve from it all. Wallowing in the pain and stress wouldn't get him anywhere. In fact, if he couldn't force his thoughts away from pursuing the subject, he might as well go back home. At least there he'd have something to do, which meant his mind was less likely to go over the whole sorry situation in a never-ending loop.

He finished his pint and immediately waved the bartender over to order another one. Too bad he couldn't allow himself to get drunk. But he'd tried going through the early morning routine with Danny while hungover once, and it wasn't something he wanted to repeat.

"That's quite a frown you've got on your face, mate."

Shane glanced up from the spot on the counter he'd apparently switched his attention to at some point and turned to his left, only to discover he needed to tilt his head back in order to look the man who'd addressed him in the face. *Fuck, the geezer is big.* At a loss about what to say in response to what was clearly a statement of fact, Shane took his time to study the man-mountain smiling down at him. He had to be at least two meters tall, with broad shoulders and a wide chest. Shane didn't think there was a lot of fat on that body though—just bones and muscle.

"You're on your own too?" the man asked. "Mind if I join you? Drinking on my own always makes me feel kinda desperate."

"Sure." Shane nodded in the direction of the empty barstool next to him. "Help yourself." He noticed the accent and tried to place it. "Australian, are you?"

"Yeah," The man's friendly features stretched into a grin. "Thanks for getting it right, mate. I'm so tired of people asking me if I'm American, I can't begin to tell you. I'm Chris."

"Shane," he responded. "I lived in the States up to five

months ago. I knew you weren't American as soon as you opened your mouth."

Shit. Why had he said that? He didn't talk about his time in Florida with anyone—not about going there, not about coming back and not about the reasons why he'd needed to return. There was too much shame and pain in those stories to share them with others.

Shane picked up his pint while sending up a silent prayer Chris wouldn't ask him about his time on the other side of the Atlantic and thanking his lucky stars when the bartender picked that moment to come and take Chris' order.

He was nothing like the type of man Shane was normally attracted to. Sure, he liked his men tall and handsome—both of which Chris was—but Chris was too close to a bear. Shane's preference ran to slimmer builds and he wasn't a huge fan of facial hair. On the other hand, he couldn't deny that the short dark brown hair dotted with tiny hints of gray was attractive, as was the goatee which covered Chris' chin but did nothing to obscure his full lips. Glasses usually didn't do anything for Shane either but they suited Chris and made his dark gray eyes sparkle.

When Chris raised one eyebrow, Shane averted his gaze and reached for his pint, disgusted to have been caught staring. What was wrong with him? Sure, it had been a long time—too long—since he'd flirted with a man, never mind picked one up. That wasn't an excuse for looking and acting desperate though.

"Have you been in Ireland long, then?" Shane asked in the hope a conversation would distract both of them from his less than subtle perusal of Chris.

"Almost ten years," Chris answered. "Came here for a few months to visit family and just never left again."

"What made you stay?" Much to his own surprise, Shane was really curious to hear the answer to that question. "I can't imagine it was the weather."

Chris threw back his head and laughed, the sound deep and clearly genuine.

"The Irish climate is nothing to write home about, that's for sure," Chris agreed. "Mind you, the heat in Australia didn't agree with me either. If I had to choose I'd take the mild but wet weather over the oppressive heat." He winked. "I guess that's exactly what I did when I decided to stay."

The both picked up their glasses and drank in silence for a few moments.

"I like your ink," Chris said while studying Shane's arm.

Shane followed his gaze and stared at the Celtic design covering most of his right arm. "Thank you." He couldn't keep the pride out of his voice. "I designed the pattern myself."

"You did?" Surprise flashed across Chris' face before being replaced by a look of delight. "You're a tattoo artist too?"

"I am," Shane confirmed. "And since you said *too*, I guess the same is true for you?"

Chris nodded. "Yes, have been for almost fifteen years now. It's the only real job I've ever had."

Shane lowered his gaze and studied Chris' forearms, only to find no sign of a tattoo anywhere. "But you've no tattoos yourself?" Shane couldn't imagine a tattooist without art on his own body but he guessed there was a probably a first time for everything.

Chris studied his own arms for a moment before answering. "None where people can see them. My mother had issues with tattoos, among other things."

"Oh?" Shane left it hanging there in the hope Chris would say more.

"You'll need to get to know me a lot better before you find out where exactly I do have art." Chris smirked before tracing a finger along the lines of the Celtic cross on Shane's biceps.

He couldn't suppress a shudder. It had been so long — too long — since anybody had touched him in a meaningful way. "Want another pint?" Shane hated the tremble in his voice when he asked the question.

"Not right now." Chris lifted his gaze while he continued to stroke Shane's arm with his finger. He glanced over Shane's shoulder in the direction of the hallway leading to the toilets and beer garden, before quirking an eyebrow at Shane.

Shane swallowed hard before nodding and getting off his barstool. He'd no idea why he was nervous. This used to be standard fare in the past. Rushed encounters in dark corners and quick fucks in the rooms of men he'd forget as soon as he left had been his normal until recently. Why the fuck did it suddenly feel like a big deal?

He forced himself to walk slowly, all too aware of the presence behind him. When he slowed down as they neared the toilets a soft push against his lower back made him continue through the backdoor and into the balmy August evening air. When he came to a standstill, Chris leaned into him and whispered in his ear. "Just around the corner there."

Glancing to the right, he saw the small path and followed it until they'd rounded the corner and found themselves in a side garden. He opened his mouth to ask where to go next and forgot the question when Chris grabbed his shoulder, pulled him around and shoved him up against the wall. Shane's heart skipped a beat as he realized he was all alone with a man big enough to squash him if he felt like it. He forced himself to meet Chris' gaze and got caught in the hungry, heated stare from his eyes.

"I..."

Chris lowered his head and captured Shane's lips with his. Since he'd no idea what he would have said if he'd been allowed to finish his sentence, Shane didn't even pretend to object and allowed himself to respond with equal urgency. It *had* been too long. It felt too good. He'd hardly ever kissed the men he'd picked up in the past—the short-lived encounters he preferred had never warranted that level of intimacy. Right now, he couldn't for the life of him remember why that had ever made sense.

He closed his eyes and lost himself in the play of their lips, relishing the way Chris' goatee scratched and tickled his clean-shaven chin. The small sounds escaping his mouth and betraying his need should have embarrassed him but only spurred him on. Given that Chris' hand was suddenly on his crotch, unzipping his fly, he imagined the feeling was mutual.

Shane's mind switched off. He'd always been the one to take charge and control of proceedings in the past. Tonight he was more than happy to relinquish control to the big Australian—delighted to just take whatever happened to be on offer. Warm air brushed across the skin of his hard and now released cock and he shuddered. The sound of a second zip opening took him by surprise, but he resisted the temptation to open his eyes. When a large hand surrounded his dick and pressed it against an equally rigid cock, he opened his mouth wider and released a groan which felt as though it came from his toes, grateful that Chris' mouth, still crushing his, captured most of the sound.

Shane was dimly aware that Chris' hand was big enough to fully encircle both their cocks. The first few strokes, the way their dicks rubbed off each other and the slight squeezes and twists Chris applied drove Shane mad. He could already feel his balls drawing up and knew he wouldn't last long. The thought shot through his head that he should ask Chris to slow down but he couldn't make himself pull back from their never-ending kiss. His orgasm roared through his body, satisfying him in ways a solitary hand job had never been able to do. Chris didn't stop his movements and stroked Shane through his orgasm and beyond until Shane's knees didn't feel strong enough to hold him up anymore.

"Fuck yeah." Chris mumbled the heartfelt words against Shane's lips as he too erupted.

The kiss ended as soon as Chris' orgasm had passed. For a moment he pulled Shane close, holding both of them up as they regained their breath and Shane managed to find a semblance of his equilibrium again. When Chris released him, pushing his softening dick back into his pants and zipping up, Shane did the same. He'd no idea why he felt both fully satisfied and deeply disappointed and ignored the question. This encounter had been more and much better than anything he could have hoped for. He'd be a fool to question it.

When Chris turned and walked back in the direction of the entrance to the pub, Shane followed.

"Thirsty work," Chris said without turning around.

Shane tried to swallow and found his throat was uncomfortably dry. "Yes, thirsty work indeed. I guess that means you're ready for that pint now?"

More books from Pride Publishing

Book one in the Dublin Virtues series

Patience is a virtue. But what if you wait too long?

Broken to be whole…

Fiction and reality become intertwined when a young movie actor playing the role of a detective finds himself in a real-life drama that threatens to bring a sudden end to his career.

Book one in the Anthem trilogy

An ocean of possibility. For love, revenge and murder.

About the Author

Helena Stone

Helena Stone can't remember a life before words and reading. After growing up in a household where no holiday or festivity was complete without at least one new book, it's hardly surprising she now owns more books than shelf space while her Kindle is about to explode.

The urge to write came as a surprise. The realisation that people might enjoy her words was a shock to say the least. Now that the writing bug has well and truly taken hold, Helena can no longer imagine not sharing the characters in her head and heart with the rest of the world.

Having left the hustle and bustle of Amsterdam for the peace and quiet of the Irish Country side she divides her time between reading, writing, long and often wet walks with the dog, her part-time job in a library, a grown-up daughter and her ever loving and patient husband.

Helena Stone loves to hear from readers. You can find contact information, website details and an author profile page at https://www.pride-publishing.com/